P9-CAM-849

JESSI'S BABY-SITTER

**Other books by
Ann M. Martin**

*Rachel Parker, Kindergarten Show-off
Eleven Kids, One Summer
Ma and Pa Dracula
Yours Turly, Shirley
Ten Kids, No Pets
Slam Book
Just a Summer Romance
Missing Since Monday
With You and Without You
Me and Katie (the Pest)
Stage Fright
Inside Out
Bummer Summer*

BABY-SITTERS LITTLE SISTER series
THE BABY-SITTERS CLUB mysteries
THE BABY-SITTERS CLUB series

JESSI'S BABY-SITTER

Ann M. Martin

AN
APPLE
PAPERBACK

SCHOLASTIC INC.
New York Toronto London Auckland Sydney

*This book is dedicated
to the memory of
Eugene Dougherty,
who taught me how to
make writing exciting.*

Cover art by Hodges Soileau

*If you purchased this book without a cover, you should be aware that this book
is stolen property. It was reported as "unsold and destroyed" to the publisher,
and neither the author nor the publisher has received any payment for this
"stripped book."*

No part of this publication may be reproduced in whole or in part,
or stored in a retrieval system, or transmitted in any form or by any
means, electronic, mechanical, photocopying, recording, or otherwise, without written permission of the publisher. For information
regarding permission, write to Scholastic Inc., 555 Broadway, New
York, NY 10012.

ISBN 0-590-73285-4

Copyright © 1990 by Ann M. Martin. All rights reserved. Published
by Scholastic Inc. THE BABY-SITTERS CLUB, THE BABY-SITTERS
CLUB logo, APPLE PAPERBACKS, and the APPLE PAPERBACKS
logo are registered trademarks of Scholastic Inc.

12 11 10 9 8 7 6 5 4 3 2 1   5   6 7 8 9/9 0 1/0

Printed in the U.S.A.   40

CHAPTER 1

"*Plié* first pozeetion, *plié* second pozeetion — nice and slowly — *plié* sird pozeetion, *plié* fourse pozeetion — *veeerry* slowly — *plié* fifs pozeetion . . . and . . . stop. . . . Non, non, non!" cried Madame Noelle. "Do not fall to zee floor. Come to a nice, graceful stop like zee lovely ballerinas you are. Now, once again."

We *pliéed* in all the pozeetions again and then came to a nice, graceful stop, even though I — and every other student in my class — just wanted to lie down and sleep for a week. We had been working hard.

I am Jessica Ramsey, otherwise known as Jessi. I am eleven years old. I am in sixth grade at Stoneybrook Middle School (SMS). In case you can't tell, I am also a dancer. (Or as Madame Noelle would say, a doncer.) I live in Stoneybrook, Connecticut, but I take ballet lessons at a special school in Stamford, another

Connecticut town (actually, a city), which isn't too far from home.

Ballet is a very important part of my life. Maybe I will go to a dance school in New York City. Maybe I will even become a professional dancer.

Class ended that day when my friends and I did not keel over after the last round of *pliés*. We changed out of our toe shoes (I am proud to say that I can dance *en pointe*), and slipped jeans or skirts over our leotards. Then we waited for our parents to pick us up.

Usually my mom comes to get me, but that day I waited and waited. Finally, fifteen minutes after everyone else had left, my dad drove up. He works in Stamford, but my lessons usually end long before he's ready to leave the office.

I ran to his car.

"Daddy!" I cried. "How come *you're* picking me up? Where's Mama? Did something happen to Becca or Squirt?"

Becca is my younger sister. She's eight. Squirt is my baby brother. His real name is John Philip Ramsey, Jr., but since he was the smallest baby in the hospital when he was born, the nurses started calling him Squirt. And the name stuck, even though now Squirt is the same size as most other toddlers his age.

2

Daddy smiled at me. "Don't worry," he said, as I slid into the front seat of the car. "Everyone's fine. I decided to leave work early today, so I called your mother and told her I'd bring you home. It would be silly for her to make the trip when I'm already here."

"Why'd you leave early?" I wanted to know. And just then a smell (well, not a smell; a wonderful chocolaty aroma) drifted to me. I turned around and saw a white bakery box on the backseat. "Hey, what's that?"

"You're certainly full of questions today," remarked Daddy. "Let's see. I left early because we have something to celebrate tonight, and the box in the backseat is part of the celebration."

"A celebration? Oh, goody!" I cried, reaching for the box.

"No peeking," said Daddy.

"But I want to see what's in there."

"The celebration is a surprise. You'll find out all about it after dinner."

I couldn't help guessing. "You got a promotion!" I exclaimed.

Daddy shook his head.

"You got a raise."

"Nope."

"We're moving back to New Jersey?"

I wasn't quite as excited by that idea. The

funny thing is, a few months ago, I would have jumped at the chance to leave Stoney-brook and return to Oakley, New Jersey, the town in which I grew up. My family and I had been happy there. We are black, and our neighborhood, school, and even my ballet school in Oakley were all mixed up — black people and white people, living and working together. Plus, my relatives lived nearby. One of my cousins, Keisha, was my best friend. When Daddy's company offered him a better job in Stamford, he jumped at the chance. But it meant we had to move. I did not want to leave Oakley. But I was not prepared for what would greet us in Stoneybrook — prejudice, that's what. We moved to a town with only a few black residents. I am the only black student in the entire sixth grade. People teased my family. People said nasty things to us. People ignored us.

At first.

Slowly, though, a change came about. I made some friends. They became good friends. Becca and I each made a best friend. Now I can't see going back to Oakley. I'd have to leave too many memories behind — like my baby-sitting adventures. Or the time our whole school went on a trip to a ski lodge in

Vermont. Or the time my friends and I went to summer camp.

But luckily Daddy said, "No, we're not moving."

Then it struck me. "You're having a baby, aren't you? You and Mama are having a *ba*by! Oh, I hope it's another boy. Then our family would be even. Two girls, two boys."

Dadddy chuckled. "It's not a new baby, either," he said. "And why don't you stop guessing? I'm afraid I'll give it away if you really do guess it."

"Okay," I said, but I continued guessing in my head. We had won the lottery. We were taking a trip to Disney World — or maybe even Texas. I had always wanted to see Texas. Then I got another idea. I bet Mama and Daddy really were having a baby, but Daddy was too smart to let on.

All the way to Stoneybrook, I hugged the secret to myself. As soon as Daddy parked the car in the driveway, I ran inside and straight to Becca's room.

"Guess what! Guess what!" I cried.

Becca looked up from her third-grade homework. "What?"

"Daddy brought a cake home and he says we're celebrating something tonight, but he won't say what. You know what I think, though? I think Mama and Daddy are going to have another baby!"

"You *do*?" Becca's eyes widened.

"Yup. I really do."

I was wrong. After dinner that evening, Daddy brought out the cake. When he had cut it and served it, he said, "We have something wonderful to celebrate."

I glanced at Becca. She glanced back, trying not to smile.

"Your mother — " Daddy began.

"I knew it! I knew it!" I cried.

"You knew that your mother found a job?" Daddy asked me.

"I — I — Mama found a job?" I repeated.

Mama was grinning away at the end of the dining room table. "That's right," she said. "It's time for me to go back to work. I was in advertising before you girls were born, and at last I can go back to that. I'm really looking forward to it. My job starts on Monday. Five days a week. Nine to five, probably longer days every now and then."

Becca and I knew how important this was to Mama, so we cheered, jumped up from our places at the table, and ran to hug her.

Then I said, settling down again, "Boy, I

guess you'll really need me to baby-sit now. I'll take care of Becca and Squirt every afternoon that I can. But who will watch Squirt while I'm at school? And who will baby-sit while I'm at my dance lessons? And, hey! Who will *drive* me to ballet class?"

Mama and Daddy exchanged a glance. I didn't like the look of it.

"What?" I asked. "What is it?"

"Well," Daddy began, and cleared his throat, "your mother will need more than just a sitter. She won't have time to shop or cook or car pool or take care of the house. So . . . um . . . so your Aunt Cecelia is going to move in. In a couple of weeks."

"Aunt Cecelia!" cried Becca and I at the same time. "Nooo!!"

Aunt Cecelia is absolutely awful. I can't tell you how many things are wrong with her. She may be Daddy's older sister, but she smells funny. Bad perfume, probably. And she is bossy and mean and thinks Mama and Daddy don't raise Becca and Squirt and me right. She thinks they let us run wild, which couldn't be farther from the truth. See, what happened was that not long ago, Mama and Daddy went away on a three-day weekend. They left me in charge, since we had a mini-vacation from school. It was the first time I'd been allowed to baby-sit overnight. Unfortunately, Becca had been invited to go sailing on Saturday — and the boats got caught in a storm, and Becca and the others were stranded on an island off the coast of Connecticut for two days. No one knew where they were. Aunt Cecelia came to stay until the crisis was over, and she was appalled that Mama and Daddy had left me in charge of Becca and Squirt.

She thought something was seriously wrong with our family.

I think she also wanted a family to live with, since her husband had died recently, and she was all alone in the house she'd moved to in Queenstown, Connecticut, after she found that she couldn't bear to stay in her home in Oakley. The house had too many memories.

This is my Aunt Cecelia: bossy, strict, mean.

Becca and I cannot stand her. And now she would be *living* with us. She would be caring for Squirt, cooking, and helping with the housework. She would also be . . . my baby-sitter. I am far too old and responsible to need a baby-sitter. After all, I'm a sitter myself.

But Aunt Cecelia does not trust me. She thinks it was my fault that Becca got lost at sea, even though Mama and Daddy gave Becca permission to go on the sailing trip.

When the "celebration" was over, Becca and I huddled in my room.

"Can you *believe* this?" I asked her. "Aunt Cecelia coming here. Moving *in*. This is a nightmare."

"A triple nightmare," agreed Becca. "Maybe we could talk Mama and Daddy out of letting her come."

"I don't think so," I said. "But I bet we could fix it so that Aunt Cecelia wouldn't want to stay once she got here. You know, put shaving cream in her slippers, a fake spider on her pillow."

"Honey in her hairbrush!" cried Becca.

"Shh!" I hissed. "That's a great idea, but keep your voice down. We don't want Mama and Daddy to know what we're up to."

CHAPTER 2

Becca and I plotted about a dozen ways to get Aunt Cecelia to leave. Most of them were very mean. We wrote them on a list, which I hid way back in my desk drawer.

Then Becca left.

I sat on my bed and felt depressed for awhile. Then I did what I always do in a tough situation.

I called my best friend, Mallory Pike.

Ring, ring went the Pikes' phone.

"Hello?" said a voice. It was Nicky, Mal's brother. (Mal has *seven* younger brothers and sisters.)

"Hi, Nicky. It's Jessi. Is Mal home?"

"Yup."

"Well, can I speak to her, please?"

"Maybe."

"*Nicky.*"

"Okay, okay, okay. . . . Oh, wait a second.

I just remembered. Mal isn't here after all. She went to the store with Mom."

"Could you have her call me back, please?" I asked. "I really need to talk to her. This is a matter of life and death . . . sort of."

"Life and death?" repeated Nicky. "Gosh."

We got off the phone. I went back to my room. I closed the door. Then I opened my door again and hung a sign on it that I'd made. The sign read (in big bold letters):

KEEP OUT (please)
THIS MEANS YOU
PRIVACY NEEDED
(THANK YOU FOR YOUR COOPERATION)

Mallory thinks the sign is dumb. She says that if you want people to stay out of your room, you should put up a sign that just says: STAY OUT OR ELSE.

I think one reason Mal is my best friend is because I like her family. The Pikes are very open and loose. There are not too many rules in the Pike house, even though there are a lot of kids. Here's who's in Mal's family, besides Mal and her parents: Byron, Adam, and Jordan, who are *identical triplets* (they're ten years

11

old); Vanessa, who's nine, very dreamy, and wants to be a poet; Nicky, who's eight, and gets pushed around by his big brothers; Margo, who's seven, and likes to tease; and Claire, who's five, the baby of the family, and seems to be stuck in a silly stage. She calls everybody "silly-billy-goo-goo."

At the Pikes', something is always going on. With eight kids, I guess that's not surprising. Anyway, Mal's household sure is different from mine. Even so, Mallory and I are alike in many ways. We're both the oldest in our families, but we feel that our parents won't let us grow up fast enough. We practically had to kick and scream in order to be allowed to get our ears pierced. Then Mal, who wears glasses, asked if she could have contacts, but her parents said no. They think she's too young. (Furthermore, Mal now has braces, so she isn't feeling particularly pretty these days, despite her pierced ears.) As for me, well, talk about being treated like a baby. Now Aunt Cecelia was going to move in. I would have a *baby*-sitter — and I'm a sitter myself!

Mal and I also have some fun things in common. We both love to read. Our favorite books are horse stories, especially the ones by Marguerite Henry, such as *Misty of Chincoteague* and *Stormy, Misty's Foal*. Mal likes to write, too. She's kept journals for years and recently talked me into keeping one as well.

However, we do have our differences. As you know, I want to be a ballerina one day (I think), but Mal wants to be an author and illustrator of children's books. The other difference is pretty obvious, I guess — our looks. Mal is white, with red hair and freckles, and she's about average height. I'm black, with long eyelashes (Mama is jealous of them) and long, *long* legs. I'm lucky to have those legs for dancing.

I'm also lucky to have found a best friend in Stoneybrook, especially after leaving Keisha behind in Oakley, but I feel even luckier to have made other friends as well. It's always nice to have a group of friends, I thought, as I settled down for a good daydream. And my group of friends are the members of the Baby-sitters Club.

I guess I haven't mentioned the BSC yet, have I? Well, the BSC consists of seven girls who have a business to do baby-sitting in our neighborhoods. We meet three times a week and get lots of sitting jobs. Mal and I are both members — junior officers. We feel honored to be part of the club, because the other members are all thirteen-year-old eighth-graders.

Kristy Thomas is the club president. Her

family is as big as the Pikes', but it is much more mixed up. Let's see. How do I even begin to tell you about her family? I guess I should start a year or so ago when Kristy was living on Bradford Court in the house she'd grown up in. She lived with her mom; her older brothers, Sam and Charlie; and her little brother, David Michael. Her father had walked out on her family not long after David Michael was born. Kristy rarely heard from him. (She still doesn't.) Anyway, the summer after seventh grade, Kristy's mom married this guy she'd been dating. His name is Watson Brewer and he's a millionaire. Honest. Watson moved Kristy's family into his mansion across town. That was when things began getting confusing. Watson has two children (Karen, who just turned seven, and Andrew, who's four) from his first marriage. Karen and Andrew live with their father every other weekend. Then, not long ago, the Brewers adopted Emily Michelle, a two-year-old Vietnamese girl. And *then*, Nannie, Kristy's grandmother, moved in to help take care of Emily Michelle. (Nannie is not a thing like Aunt Cecelia. She's nice.) The Brewers also have a dog and a cat.

Kristy is nice but bossy. She's a tomboy, and she coaches a team of little kids who like to play softball. She is *full* of ideas. (She started

14

the Baby-sitters Club.) Kristy is also just a little immature compared to her friends. She's not too interested in clothes yet, she *never* wears makeup, and she doesn't date. But she does like a boy in her neighborhood! His name is Bart and he's very nice.

Kristy's best friend is Mary Anne Spier, the secretary of the club. Kristy and Mary Anne are similar to Mal and me in that they're very alike in some ways and very different in others. For one thing, they look a little alike. They both have brown eyes and brown hair and are short. (Kristy is shorter.) And Mary Anne used to dress in a babyish way, but now she cares much more about clothes than she used to. I think the similarities end there. Mary Anne is quiet and shy — although she's the only one of us to have a steady boyfriend. Her boyfriend is Logan Bruno, and he's actually part of the BSC, but I'll explain how later. Mary Anne's family used to be as different from Kristy's as you could imagine, but now it has changed. See, Mary Anne's mom died when Mary Anne was really little, so Mary Anne grew up an only child living with her dad, who was quite strict. Then Mr. Spier met an old high-school girlfriend of his (who was divorced by then), and after a pretty long time, they finally got married. Guess who the girl-

15

friend was — the mother of Dawn Schafer, another club member, and Mary Anne's other best friend. Dawn, her brother, and her mom had moved back to Stoneybrook (they'd been living in California) after the Schafers' divorce. Dawn and Mary Anne got to be friends, then their parents began dating, and now the best friends are stepsisters, too. They all live in Dawn's house, which is a colonial farmhouse.

Dawn is *so* cool. (Or, as Claudia Kishi, another BSC member, would say, she's *fresh*.) Dawn has long pale blonde hair that reaches halfway down her back. Her eyes are sparkling blue. She dresses in a casual style all her own. And, although she likes Stoneybrook and her new family, she longs for California — for a couple of reasons. In the first place, she was raised there. She misses the house she grew up in, the warmer climate, and of course, her father. She also misses her brother. That's right. Jeff is back in California, living with Mr. Schafer. He just never adjusted to Connecticut the way Dawn did. He had trouble in school and he wasn't happy. So he returned to California. At first Dawn felt terrible. She felt as if her family had been ripped in two. Now that she's got a stepfather and a stepsister (not to mention a kitten — Mary Anne's), she feels more complete. But she still visits her father and Jeff whenever she can.

Things at the Schafer/Spier home got off to a troubled start after the wedding. Dawn and Mary Anne were friends, but they weren't prepared to be stepsisters. And Dawn and her mom are as different from Mary Anne and her dad as night and day. They have varying ideas on everything from meals to housecleaning. But they're overcoming things. I think that deep down, Dawn and Mary Anne are happy to be stepsisters.

Let's see. The two remaining BSC members are Claudia Kishi, club vice-president, and Stacey McGill, club treasurer. Claudia and Stacey are best friends and also have their similarities and differences. (I guess all best friends do.) Both Claudia and Stacey are pretty *fresh* themselves. They are the most sophisticated of all us members. None of us usually comes right out and says that, but we all know it's true.

Claudia comes from a regular family. It's like mine, I guess. She lives with her parents and her older sister, Janine. Janine, however, is a genius in the true sense of the word (she has this amazingly high I.Q.), while Claudia, who's smart, is a terrible student. She simply doesn't like school. (Oh, and she's an awful speller.) What she does like is art, and is she ever talented. Claud can sculpt, paint, draw, you name it. She even makes wild jewelry to go with her wild clothes. Claud wears things my mother won't even let me *look* at in stores — short, short skirts and tight black pants and off-the-shoulder sweat shirts. Also, she can think of a thousand ways to wear her hair, which is long, silky, and jet-black. Claud is Japanese-American and very exotic-looking. She's also fun. She loves to read Nancy Drew mysteries and eat junk food, but her parents don't approve of either habit. Does that deter Claudia? No. She just hides the books and food all around her room. Once, I dropped a pencil on her floor and it rolled under an armchair. I reached down to pick it up, and my hand closed over a Planters Peanut Bar! Claud likes boys and goes out on dates and to school dances, but she doesn't have one special boyfriend yet. Here's one sad thing about Claudia. Her grandmother Mimi used to live with her family. I think Claudia was closer to Mimi than to anyone else in the world. Then Mimi got sick and died. That was a hard time for all of us, but especially for Claud.

And now we come to Stacey. Stacey shares Claudia's sense of fashion and, if this is possible, she's even more sophisticated than

Claud. Her mother lets her perm her hair, she has pierced ears (well, so do all of us, except for Kristy and Mary Anne), and her clothes are even more cool than Claudia's. I think. Actually, maybe they're about even on the coolness scale.

But there's one thing about Stacey that none of us can top: she grew up in New York City. Big, thrilling, exciting New York City, the shopping capital of the world. How did Stacey wind up in Stoneybrook? Well, the company Mr. McGill works for transferred his job to Stamford, so Stacey and her parents settled in Stoneybrook. (Stacey is an only child.) Then, after they'd been here about a year, Mr. McGill was transferred *back* to New York. (When they left, they sold their house — to my family!) Anyway, that was when the trouble started. Mr and Mrs. McGill began having problems. Finally, they separated. Mrs. McGill wanted to move back here, while Mr. McGill stayed in the city. It was a tough decision, but Stacey finally chose to live with her mom in Stoneybrook. (Boy, were we glad to have her back.) So Stacey's life might seem glamorous, but it hasn't been easy. Especially when you consider that on top of everything else, Stacey has a disease called diabetes. She has to stay on a strict no-sweets diet and give herself (oh, *ew*)

19

daily injections of something called insulin. All in all, though, Stacey copes pretty well, even when she isn't feeling too great. And she's a very good friend to all of us.

The phone rang then, and it jolted me out of my daydream. I jumped off my bed. I hadn't begun my homework. I hadn't practiced at my *barre* in the basement, either. Even so, I hoped the phone call was from Mallory. Homework or not, practice or not, all I wanted to do was pour out the story of Aunt Cecelia to my best friend.

CHAPTER 3

"'Bye, Mama!" I called. "I'm going to Claudia's for the meeting. I'll be back in time for dinner!"

"Have fun, sweetie," my mother replied.

I dashed into our garage, hopped on my bike, and rode toward Claud's house, hurrying. It is never a good idea to be late for a meeting. Kristy feels it is her presidential duty to run the BSC meetings in as official a manner as possible. So I pedaled along quickly.

On the way I thought about how nice it was to have Mama at home. I'd never thought about it before; I guess because there was no reason to think of her *not* being there. Even when she began to job-hunt, I didn't think what it would be like to have two working parents. It didn't seem real enough.

But now that Mama would soon *not* be at home, I spent a good deal of time appreciating having her around. It was nice to return from

21

school and find her in the den, paying bills; or on the phone, doing volunteer work; or best of all, in the kitchen, baking cookies with Squirt at her heels. Soon all that would be over. I'd come home to . . . Aunt Cecelia. (I always imagined scary music playing when I thought of her name.) And when I left for a club meeting, I would have to call good-bye to . . . Aunt Cecelia.

My own baby-sitter.

I pulled into Claud's driveway and parked my bicycle by a lamppost. Then I let myself into the Kishis' house. There's no point in ringing the bell, because both Mr. and Mrs. Kishi work, and Janine often isn't at home, so us club members just run upstairs instead of making Claudia come downstairs when we know perfectly well where to go.

"Hi!" I said when I entered Claud's room.

Claudia, Kristy, and Dawn were there, in their usual places. I took *my* usual place.

"Hi, Jessi!" my friends replied.

Claud and Dawn were sitting on Claud's bed, leaning against the wall. Kristy was perched in the director's chair, which she has claimed as her own — the president's throne. She was wearing a visor, and a pencil was stuck over one ear.

I sat on the floor. We were waiting for Mallory, Stacey, and Mary Anne. While we waited, I only half listened to the others, who were talking loudly. I couldn't help thinking about Aunt Cecelia, about how Mama and Daddy had gotten me a *baby-sitter*. And then I began to think about our own sitting club.

This is how the BSC got started. It all began more than a year ago, when Kristy, Claudia, Mary Anne, and Stacey were new seventh-grade students at SMS. I still lived in New Jersey then, Dawn still lived in California, and Mal was a lowly fifth-grader at Stoneybrook Elementary. She wasn't even a sitter yet.

Anyway, back then, Kristy lived across the street from Claud, and Mary Anne lived next door to her. The three of them had grown up together and all liked to baby-sit, but they did their sitting on their own. Then one day Kristy's mom (who was just beginning to date Watson Brewer) needed a sitter for David Michael, who was only six. No one was available — not Kristy, not Sam or Charlie, not any of the sitters Mrs. Thomas had phoned. It was while Kristy was watching her mother make all those telephone calls that she got what was probably the most brilliant idea of her life. Wouldn't it be easy if her mom could make just *one* call and reach a lot of sitters at once? Of course it would!

So she told Claudia and Mary Anne about her idea for a sitting business, and they formed the Baby-sitters Club. They asked Stacey to join, too. She and Claud were already getting to be friends, and the girls thought that four sitters would be better than three. That was the start of the BSC.

The club did well from the beginning, thanks partly to all the advertising the girls did and partly to the fact that they were (and still are) excellent sitters, so people asked them back after they'd done a good job. Soon the BSC business was booming, and when Dawn moved to town, they asked her to join. Everything went smoothly until Stacey had to move back to New York. By then, a year had gone by, the original club members were in eighth grade, and Mal had joined them at SMS as a sixth-grader. She was old enough to sit (and she certainly had plenty of experience with young children), so they asked both Mal and me to replace Stacey. Then, of course, Stacey moved back here (I felt guilty that she couldn't move into her old house, since we were living in it), and she settled into the club routine again. We have seven members now, and Kristy says that's enough. I think she's right. Claud's bedroom is getting crowded.

How does the club run? Well, we meet three

times a week, on Monday, Wednesday, and Friday afternoons from 5:30 until 6:00. People know that we meet then and they call us to line up sitters. They also know to call us at Claudia's, whose bedroom is BSC headquarters.

Kristy, as I mentioned, is our president. Her job is to conduct meetings, solve problems, get good ideas, and generally keep things running smoothly. These are two of Kristy's ideas: Kid-Kits, and the club notebook. Kid-Kits are terrific. Kristy suggested that we each get a cardboard carton, decorate it, and fill it with things kids like to play with — our old books, games, and toys, plus stickers, coloring books, and art materials. We sometimes take the Kid-Kits with us when we baby-sit, and children *love* them. This is good for business, because when our charges are happy, then their parents are happy, and then the parents ask us to sit again.

The club notebook is a good idea, too, but not nearly as much fun. In it, each of us has to write up every single job we go on. I think that's a royal pain, but I have to admit it's helpful. See, once a week we're supposed to read the notebook to see what happened while our friends were sitting, and often I find out how they solved tough sitting situations, or learn about a problem a kid is having whom I'll be sitting for soon.

Claudia is the vice-president because we're always using (or eating) her things. Three times a week we take over her room. We tie up her phone and we eat her junk food. Claud is pretty good-natured about this. In fact, I think she likes having us come over.

The job of the secretary, Mary Anne, is a big one. Mary Anne is in charge of the club *record* book (not the notebook), in which she keeps track of our clients, their addresses and phone numbers, and the rates they pay. More importantly, she schedules every single one of our sitting jobs. She has to keep track of all our other activities and appointments, such as my ballet lessons, Mal's orthodontist appointments, and Kristy's softball practices. I do not think Mary Anne has ever made a mistake.

Stacey is our treasurer. She's good with numbers. It's her job to keep a record of the money we earn (just for our interest), to collect dues from each of us every Monday, to preside over the treasury, and to dole out money when it's needed — to help Claudia pay for her phone bill, to replace items in the Kid-Kits that get used up, such as crayons, and to shell out for a club pizza party or slumber party every now and then. The funny thing is, Stacey loves collecting money — *having* it — but hates parting with it, even though it isn't her own. Nothing pleases her more than the sight of a fat treasury envelope.

Dawn is our alternate officer. That means that if one of us has to miss a meeting, Dawn can take over that person's job. She's sort of like an understudy in a play. She has to know how to handle the treasury, schedule appointments, etc.

Then there are Mal and me. As junior officers, we take on a lot of the afternoon sitting jobs. This is mostly because we aren't allowed to sit at night yet unless we're sitting for our own brothers and sisters. But it does free the other girls up for nighttime jobs, so all in all we're important club members, too.

Believe it or not, there are a couple of other club members whom I haven't described yet. This is because they are associate members and don't come to meetings. They are our backups. They're responsible sitters we can call on if a job comes up that none of us seven regular members can take, which does happen sometimes. Our associate members are Shannon Kilbourne, a friend of Kristy's, and . . . Logan Bruno, Mary Anne's boyfriend!

                              *   *   *

"Ahem," said Kristy loudly.

I looked up guiltily. Boy, had I been day-dreaming. The rest of the BSC members had arrived and Kristy was starting the meeting. She took role. Then Stacey collected our dues, gleefully exclaiming over the contents of the treasury and beaming when no one said they needed any money. After that, we waited for job calls to come in.

The first was from Mrs. Rodowsky. She and her husband have three boys — Shea, Jackie, and Archie. Jackie, the seven-year-old, is a walking disaster, completely accident-prone, but we love him.

I got the job.

When the phone didn't ring again for awhile, we began talking.

"When's your aunt coming, Jessi?" Stacey wanted to know. (By then, practically the whole world knew my aunt was moving in.)

"I'm not sure," I said. "I mean, Aunt Cecelia isn't even sure. She still has to hire movers, sell some of her furniture, things like that." I paused. Then, "Ohhh," I moaned. "*Why* does she have to come? There must be some other solution to this problem. Perhaps my parents could hire a jailer."

Kristy giggled. But then she said, "Really,

Jessi. How bad could having your aunt move in actually be? Nannie moved in with my family, and it's been great. We love having her around."

"And Mimi lived with us for as long as I can remember," added Claud. "You know how I felt about her. She was like another mother."

I knew. And I knew that Nannie was wonderful, too.

But Aunt Cecelia would not be wonderful, and my friends wouldn't understand that until they personally saw Aunt Cecelia in action.

CHAPTER 4

Wednesday

Well, here we go again.
Another afternoon with
Jackie Rodowsky, the
walking disaster.
Actually, I have to
admit that this time
he wasn't much of
a klutz. Only a few
little things happened.
What was interesting
is that Jackie decided
to enter the science
fair. And he wants
to do a very
interesting project.
Have you ever seen
those miniature erupting
volcanoes? Jackie wants
to build one. (Leave

it to Jackie to choose the messiest possible project!) What have I gotten myself into?

I raced directly to the Rodowskys' from school. Mrs. Rodowsky needed me by three-thirty so that she could drive Shea to his music lesson and little Archie to his soccer lesson. (Can you imagine a bunch of four-year-olds playing soccer? It must be quite a sight.)

As I pedaled along, I remembered telling Mama that morning that I would be going directly to a sitting job after school. I knew she wouldn't worry about me. But, I thought, would things be different when Aunt Cecelia was in charge? Would she let me go places without checking in after school? Would she remember my afternoon plans when I told them to her over breakfast in the morning?

Aunt Cecelia is an old prune.

I arrived at the Rodowsky's right on time, parked my bike, and rang their front doorbell.

I heard running footsteps inside, then a whoosh, a crash, and a cry of, "Oh, darn, darn. Oh . . . *bull*frogs!"

I giggled. I knew that was Jackie.

"Jackie!" I called. "It's me, Jessi. Are you okay?"

Jackie opened the door, looking sheepish. "I was running to answer the bell and I slipped on the rug and fell on my bottom."

I smiled, shaking my head. Then I let myself in and helped Jackie straighten out the rug.

"Jessi?" called Mrs. Rodowsky. "Is that you?"

"Yes!" I replied. (I hoped she didn't think *I* had slipped on the rug.)

Mrs. Rodowsky was in a rush.

"Archie!" she exclaimed. "You're supposed to be in your soccer uniform. And, Shea, where are your piano books?"

The house was in turmoil for about five minutes — Jackie added to it by somehow getting his foot stuck in one of his old rain boots — but finally Mrs. R. and the boys were backing hurriedly down the driveway. I was left with Jackie and the rain boot.

"I know I can get this off your foot," I told him.

"But what if you can't?" whimpered Jackie.

"Jackie," I said, "have you ever heard of someone who got a boot stuck on his foot and *never* got it off?"

"No," replied Jackie, as I braced myself against a wall and pulled.

"I wonder," said Jackie, trying not to slide forward. "You know, boots are sometimes called galoshes. Is *one* boot called a galosh?"

"I haven't the faintest — *oof!* Well, there you go, Jackie. The boot's off. You're free."

"Thanks," he said gratefully.

Jackie wandered around the playroom, looking bored.

"What do you want to do?" I asked him.

"I don't know."

"Do you have any homework?"

"Nope. Well, not really. We're just supposed to think about whether we want to enter the science fair at school."

"Do you?" I asked him.

"*Me?*" squeaked Jackie. "Are you kidding? I have bad luck. I would never enter a contest. . . . Even though I think it would be fun to make a volcano."

"Fun to do *what?*" I repeated.

"Make a volcano. I saw that on *The Brady Bunch* once. You can build a model of a volcano, but it really works. I mean, lava really comes pouring out. That would be great. Lava everywhere."

The thought of "lava everywhere" made me sort of queasy. Even so, I said, "Jackie, you ought to make a volcano for the science fair! It would be a great project. Everyone else would probably just have, you know, things like leaf collections, or bugs in jars, but *you* would build a *volcano* that would *erupt*. You'd win for sure."

Jackie looked skeptical. "I don't know," he said. "I bet some kids would do really, really, really good projects. I'm not very smart in science. Besides, like I said, I have bad luck. I can't show a project to judges and an audience. Things never go right for me. Something bad would happen."

"Jackie. That's no way to talk. You have to have confidence in yourself. A volcano — a spewing, dripping, running volcano — is a really terrific project. The kids would love it. More important, so would the teachers and judges."

"I don't know," said Jackie slowly.

"Oh, come on," I said. "This'll be great. Let's go to the library right now and see what kind of information we can find on volcanoes and how to make them. I'll leave a note for your mom in case she comes home early."

I didn't give Jackie a chance to say no. I just handed him his jacket, wrote the note, put on my own jacket, and marched Jackie to the public library. He barely said a word as we walked along.

When we reached the library, the first person we saw was Mrs. Kishi, Claudia's mother! She's the head librarian.

"Hello," she greeted us, as we entered the children's section. "What are you two doing here?"

I explained Jackie's project to Mrs. Kishi.

"Hmm," she said, "let's look in the science section."

Claud's mom helped us find three books. One was about volcanoes, one was about earth sciences, and the third was a book of science experiments, including a chapter called "How to Make an Erupting Volcano."

"Gosh," said Jackie. "I didn't think we'd find this. It's exactly what I need. It has all the directions."

"You never know what you'll find in a library," said Mrs. Kishi, smiling. Then she left Jackie and me sitting at a table with our books.

Jackie began to read the exploding-volcano experiment. "You know," he said, "this doesn't look so easy. It says you have to make a frame out of wood and glass to put your volcano in. They didn't do that on *The Brady Bunch*."

"Well, *we're* going to," I informed him. "We're going to make the best project in your whole school."

"But there are words here I don't understand. The book says you have to get different colored clay to make ig — iggy —"

"Igneous," I supplied.

"Okay. Igneous rocks. And . . . and metal —"

"Metamorphic rocks."

"And . . . oh, boy."

"Sedimentary rocks."

"Whoa," whispered Jackie. "And then you have to get stuff called, um — "

Even I had to pause for that one. "I'm not sure what this is," I said at last.

"So where are we going to get it?" asked Jackie worriedly.

"It says you can buy it at a drugstore."

Jackie was quiet. He seemed stumped.

"What's wrong?" I asked him.

"On *The Brady Bunch* they just made a mound of papier-mâché or something and put this goo in and — *whoosh!* Why do I need to know about rocks? And why do I have to make a glass box? That sounds hard. And expensive. I just spent all my allowance."

"First of all," I replied, "like I said, we're going to make the best project in the school. I bet the volcano on *The Brady Bunch* didn't win a prize, did it?"

"No," answered Jackie triumphantly. "It was just for fun."

36

"Oh," I said. "Well, ours will be special. Plus, I'm sure your parents will help you buy the materials for your project. Now, come on. Sit next to me. I have to learn all about volcanoes first. If you want to win in the science fair, you can't just make your volcano erupt. You have to tell the judges about volcanoes."

Jackie sat next to me while I learned about lava and fire and fountains and ash and gas and some pretty disgusting things. Jackie sat next to me and looked at the volcano experiment with a frown.

After about twenty minutes, I stood up. "Well," I said, "I think I've got a handle on volcanoes now."

"Good," replied Jackie, "because I don't."

"We'll check these books out and go home."

"Oh," said Jackie, brightening. "I don't have my library card."

"Never mind. I've got mine," I told him.

So we checked out the books and walked back to Jackie's house. When Mrs. Rodowsky returned with Shea and Archie, she found Jackie and me still looking through the books. Well, Jackie was looking (sort of). I was making a list of materials he would need.

"Jackie's entering the science fair?" said Mrs. Rodowsky, after I told her what we were doing. She looked both pleased and surprised.

"Yes," I said happily.

"But, Mom, we need clay and glass and some stuff from the drugstore. It might be expensive," said Jackie.

"I don't think it will be *too* expensive," said Mrs. R. "Jackie, I'm so proud of you for wanting to work on a project. And, Jessi, thank you for inspiring him. I'm impressed that you convinced him to enter. Listen, would you mind helping Jackie with his project? The two of you seem to know what you're doing. Maybe you could arrange with the members of the Baby-sitters Club to be our only sitter between now and the science fair. That way you and Jackie will have plenty of time together."

"I think that's possible," I said. "I'll have to check with my friends, but I'm sure they'll understand."

"Great!" said Mrs. R.

I left the Rodowskys' with a smile on my face. I knew I could help Jackie all the way to a prize.

CHAPTER 5

Saturday

Today, Dawn and I sat for my younger brothers and sisters. It was a fun afternoon, wasn't it?

Definitely, Mal. Your family is really something. With eight kids, you guys can come up with pretty neat projects. I think the most ambitious thing Jeff and I ever did was set up a table in front of our house in California. We sold bunches of flowers that grew wild everywhere. Nobody bought any, of course. Oops, I'm off the subject.

That's okay. Well, to get back to our job, two things were going on. One, Margo decided to enter the Stoneybrook Elementary science fair. Two, the other Kids needed something to do so they... opened a true and actual lending library!

It was a peaceful Saturday at Mal's house. Dawn had arrived to help her baby-sit, Mr. and Mrs. Pike had just left, all of Mal's brothers and sisters were at home, and nobody was fighting. Not even Nicky and the triplets. Dawn had brought over her Kid-Kit (Mallory's is no good at her own house, since it's mostly full of the Pikes' things), and Claire, Margo, and Vanessa were looking through it. The boys were playing their endless imaginary game about the Wandering Frog People. That has been going on for about two years now, which is one year and 364 days longer than Mal had hoped it would last. At any rate, the triplets were occupied.

"Look!" said Claire, peering eagerly into Dawn's Kid-Kit. "It's the new Skipper doll. Cool! She has sleepover stuff with her."

"Here's a jigsaw puzzle," said Vanessa. "Ooh, this looks hard."

"It is," Dawn told her, "but I think you'll like it. When you put it together it's a poem.

It's the one by Robert Frost about stopping by woods on a snowy evening. And all around the poem are snowflakes."

"I'm going to try it," said Vanessa, immediately dumping the pieces onto the floor. Vanessa loves to read and write poetry.

Margo looked halfheartedly through the box. She didn't seem to want to play with anything.

"Something wrong, Margo?" Mallory asked her. Margo has the world's weakest stomach. Mallory sincerely hoped it wasn't upset.

Margo shook her head. "I'm just thinking," she replied.

"About what?" asked Dawn.

"Well, our school is having a science fair and anyone can enter."

"Do you want to enter?" asked Mal. "I entered three times when I was at Stoneybrook Elementary. I'm not great in science, but the fair was a lot of fun anyway."

"It was?" said Margo. "Maybe I'll enter, then. Our teacher said we'll get extra credit for entering. Will you help me, Mallory?"

"Sure," replied Mal. "I mean, I'll *help* you, but I won't do your project *for* you. Deal?"

"Deal," said Margo. She grinned.

"Do you have any idea what you want to do your project on?" asked Dawn.

Margo thought for awhile. "No," she said at last.

"Well, let's go upstairs and look at the books in our rooms," suggested Mallory. "We have some science books."

"Maybe we'll find the Wandering Frog People while we're at it," said Dawn, with a little smile.

Mallory looked up. The boys were gone. That wasn't much of a surprise, since Wandering Frog People is a very quiet game.

What was a surprise, though, was finding Nicky and the triplets in their room, poring over a set of encyclopedias.

"What are you doing?" Mal asked her brothers as she and Margo stopped in the doorway.

"Looking up frog stuff," replied Jordan. "Adam says there's such a thing as an African tree toad, but I don't believe him."

"Don't we have a book on reptiles somewhere?" asked Mal.

"And I need to find a book about . . . about the sky," said Margo, suddenly inspired. "I want my project to be about constellations or maybe the planets."

"What we need is a library," said Mallory.

"Hey!" exclaimed Byron. "We could make a library right here in our rooms. Altogether, we have science books; mysteries; your horse stories, Mal; Claire's picture books; the Hardy Boys and Nancy Drew books" (Adam made a face at the mention of Nancy Drew); "Vanessa's poetry books; Nicky's dog stories; and all those other books." (The Pike kids get a lot of books on their birthdays and on holidays. They like to read.)

"Yeah . . ." said Nicky slowly. "A real library. Neat."

"We could organize it like the public library," said Jordan, getting excited, too. "And we could really let kids around here borrow our books."

"We need a librarian," said Adam.

"Vanessa!" cried the others immediately. "Vanessa would be a great librarian. She's always reading or writing."

"But I have to figure out my science-fair project," said Margo. "How can I do that while you guys are having all the fun making a library?" Margo looked (and sounded) miffed.

"Easy," said the ever-practical Byron. "You help us with the library. Then, when it's all ready, you can go to the science section to work on your project. You can be our first customer."

"All *right!*" cried Margo.

"Margo, go tell Dawn and Claire and Vanessa to come up here," said Jordan. "We'll need everyone to help us."

Margo turned and faced the stairs. "DAWN! CLAIRE! VANESSA!" she yelled. "COME HERE!"

"Margo," said Mallory, giggling, "Jordan could have done *that* himself."

It wasn't long before preparations for the library were underway. Mallory and Dawn were amazed at how organized the kids, especially the older ones, were about their project.

"First," said Byron, "we have to group the same kinds of books together. We've all got science books in our rooms. They should go on the same bookshelf. Margo, you've got Bobbsey Twins books; Vanessa, you've got Nancy Drews; and Nicky and I both have Hardy Boys. We should put those mystery series in another bookcase."

"I think all the animal stories should go together, too," said Nicky.

Well, for awhile, the upstairs of the Pike house was a pretty big mess, with the kids carrying books back and forth, in and out of rooms.

"What are your parents going to say when they get home?" Dawn asked Mal, looking worried.

44

"Nothing! They'll love this!"

When the books had been organized, the kids divided themselves into four groups. Well, not exactly *groups*, since one of the groups consisted of just one person. Anyway, Vanessa, the chosen librarian, set up her desk as the checkout counter, and Claire helped her. Byron made signs that read ANIMAL STO-RIES, MYSTERIES, etc. Jordan and Margo made a huge stack of pockets to tape inside the covers of the books, and Adam and Nicky took index cards, wrote the title of one book on each card, and stuck it in the pocket that Jordan and Margo had just made. It was a real assembly line and took quite a bit of work, but by late that afternoon, the library was ready. The Pike kids looked satisfied.

Vanessa manned her desk. The others stood in the bedrooms, as library aides, Mallory guessed. And Margo announced, "Here I am! Your first customer. I need to see the science section, please."

"Right over here," said Adam, pulling his sister into the boys' room. "What are you looking for?"

"I'm not sure," replied Margo. "I guess stuff about space."

Adam handed Margo several books, she sat down at a desk, began reading, and . . .

"Now what?" asked Nicky. "Where are our other customers."

"Um, nobody else knows about your library," Dawn pointed out gently.

The Pike kids looked wounded, but just for a minute.

"We'll advertise!" said Vanessa.

"Yeah, we'll make a big sign that says 'Pike Library' and put it in the front yard!" exclaimed Jordan.

So the triplets made the sign, and then they, Nicky, and Claire went from house to house in the neighborhood, telling all their friends about the *very* local public library. They returned with Matt and Haley Braddock.

"We're bored," said Haley, who's nine. "We need some new books to read."

Actually, Haley didn't just speak. She spoke and used sign language at the same time, since Matt, who's seven, is profoundly deaf and can't speak or hear.

"Yeah," signed Matt. "I want a book about baseball."

Beaming, Nicky helped the Braddocks find their books. While they were looking, the doorbell rang. Buddy and Suzi Barrett were on the front stoop, also wanting books.

"This is great!" cried Nicky. "Our library is working!"

Vanessa was busy at the checkout desk. Whenever a customer found a book, she removed the card from the pocket, wrote on it the name of the person who was checking out the book, and also the day's date. Then she set the card aside and stuck a Post-It on the book pocket with the due date written on it.

"Overdue books cost you ten cents a day," she told each customer, "so bring them back on time."

Meanwhile, Margo had decided on her science project. "I am going to make a shadow box," she said. "It will show what life would be like if the moon was our home planet."

"Great!" said Mal.

When Mr. and Mrs. Pike returned, they were pleased with the Pike Library, but not pleased when Buddy Barrett returned his book during dinner that night. Byron had to add something to the sign in the front yard:

Open weekdays from 3:30 - 6:00 p.m.
Open weekends from 10:00 a.m. - 5:00 p.m.
Not open during meals!

CHAPTER 6

*D*um da-dum dum.

The dreaded day had arrived.

Aunt Cecelia was moving in.

It was the Saturday following the one when the Pike Library opened. And it began early. Daddy and Mama were up at the crack of dawn. So was I. I was in the basement, practicing at the *barre* Daddy had built for me, and scrutinizing my leg movements in the big mirror. But when I smelled coffee brewing in the kitchen, I went upstairs to see just how the awful day was going to start.

"She rented a U-Haul," Daddy was telling Mama as I reached the kitchen. He was scrambling eggs while Mama cut up fruit.

"A U-Haul!" exclaimed Mama.

"Well, just a small one," said Daddy. "She sold some of her things, put a lot of other things in storage, and the rest is moving here with her."

48

"Where's she going to put it all?" I asked.

"Good morning, Jessi," was Mama and Daddy's reply.

" 'Morning," I answered. I didn't say *good* morning, because it wasn't.

"She's going to put it in the guest room. That will be her room. You know that," Mama told me.

"A whole U-Haul's worth of furniture?" I pressed.

Daddy gave me a look that plainly said, "Don't push it."

So I didn't.

At eight o'clock, Daddy left for Aunt Cecelia's. He would have to attach the U-Haul to our station wagon and drive it back here while Aunt Cecelia drove her own car. I was awfully glad she had a car. That meant she wouldn't be stuck in our house day in and day out. As Kristy's big brother says, "A set of wheels is, like, totally necessary."

Daddy was gone a long time.

"He has to oversee the movers," Mama explained to Becca and me as we ate lunch (our last meal without Aunt Cecelia). "And hooking the U-Haul to our car may take a little while."

Daddy and Aunt Cecelia arrived at our house around two-thirty. Mama, Becca,

Squirt, and I were sitting on the front stoop. We were sitting under a banner that read: WELCOME, AUNT CECILIA. Mama had insisted that Becca and I make the banner, so we purposely spelled our aunt's name wrong. (Mama hadn't noticed.)

When the cars and the U-Haul pulled into our driveway, Becca and I just looked at each other. We didn't even stand up until Mama nudged us and said, "What happened to your manners?"

So we walked to the driveway, trailing behind Mama.

Aunt Cecelia got out of her car, kissed us all, and then said, "Rebecca, don't slouch," and, "Jessica, *please* tidy up your hair."

What could we say? Becca stands like any normal eight-year-old, and I'd been practicing all morning. Of course my hair was a mess.

"Well," said Daddy, sounding a little too cheerful, "let's get Aunt Cecelia's things inside." He opened up the U-Haul. It was *packed!*

I almost cried, "Where are we going to put all that stuff?" but I knew better. I just picked up a carton and lugged it inside. Becca did the same.

After about half an hour, the guest room was overflowing, and there were still two chairs, this dumb bird cage on a stand (no bird

50

in it), a little table, some lamps, a tea cart, and even a small rug in the van. Not to mention more cartons.

"Mama," I said urgently, "those things are *not* going to fit in Aunt Cecelia's room. You can barely walk around in there now."

"I know," Mama replied. "We'll find places for them."

"That's right." Aunt Cecelia had come up behind us. "A place for everything and everything in its place," she said primly.

I hadn't expected those places to be all over our house. We crammed a bunch of things, including the bird cage, into the living room. The small rug was placed over a larger rug in the den. It looked terrible. One of the tables wound up in my room.

"Mama, *why* did she bring so much stuff?" Becca whispered when Aunt Cecelia was busy in the guest room. I mean, *her* room.

"Because it belongs to her. It's part of her past," Mama replied gently. "It reminds her of her life with her husband, and she misses your Uncle Steven very much."

For a moment, I felt sorry for Aunt Cecelia. But just for a moment. The next thing I knew, she was handing me two china eggs and asking me to put them in my room because there wasn't room in hers.

When she'd gone, I looked around my room. It was changed. It didn't say "Jessi" anymore. It said "Jessi and some old lady." Our house didn't feel like our house anymore, either. Marks of Aunt Cecelia were everywhere.

Squirt was confused, and I didn't blame him one bit.

But Aunt Cecelia, looking at the not-yet-organized house said, "I'll have things in order in no time."

"I hope so," Mama replied. "I start my job on Monday."

Aunt Cecelia kept her word. By that evening, our house was tidy (but crowded), Aunt Cecelia had unpacked and put away all the stuff in her bedroom, and she'd folded the cartons, stacked them, and tied them with string for the trash man to take away on Tuesday.

"She's efficient," Daddy remarked.

"She's a drill sergeant," I whispered to Becca.

"Girls, are you ready for bed?" Aunt Cecelia called upstairs.

Ready for bed? It was too early to go to bed. And why was Aunt Cecelia calling us, anyway?

"Not yet," I replied.

"Well, please put on your nightgowns."

Becca and I looked at each other, mystified. Then we put on our nightgowns, but we went downstairs afterward to find out what Mama and Daddy were doing. Guess what. They were just sitting in the den, reading. Why weren't they stopping Aunt Cecelia?

"Mama," I whispered, "Aunt Cecelia told me to get ready for bed, and it's only eight-thirty."

"You don't have to go to bed yet," said Mama absently, but she was much more interested in her book than in the injustices Aunt Cecelia was carrying out against Becca and me.

My sister and I left the den.

"They weren't any help," said Becca.

"They're tired," I told her. "And Mama's probably enjoying this last weekend before she begins work. We should let them relax."

That was a bad move on our part.

The next morning, our family had just gotten up when Daddy said brightly, "I've got a great idea. Why don't we go out for brunch this morning? We'll celebrate your mother's new job and having my sister here with us."

"Oh, why don't you two go out alone?" Aunt Cecelia said to Daddy and Mama. "Now that I'm here, you can have a private brunch.

Wouldn't that be special? No children's menu to look at. No high chair to worry about. I'll stay here and baby-sit for Jessi and Becca and Squirt. After all, that's one reason I moved in."

Mama and Daddy were thrilled with the idea, but all I could think was, *She'll* stay here and baby-sit for *us?* On a Sunday morning? *I* could do that. I *have* done that.

But I kept my mouth shut.

So Mama and Daddy left, and Aunt Cecelia baby-sat for my sister and brother and me. And I mean, she baby-sat. She did everything for us. That's okay where Squirt's concerned, but Becca is too old to be reminded to use her napkin (she knows when to do that), and I am *much* too old to be told to clean my plate. Sometimes I can't. Besides, I have to watch my weight. I can't be a fat ballerina.

When our breakfast was finally over, I lifted Squirt out of his high chair and began to clean him up like I always do.

"I'll take care of that," said Aunt Cecelia. "You girls get dressed."

As Becca and I dragged ourselves upstairs, I said to my sister, "I've got a new name for Aunt Cecelia."

"What?" asked Becca.

"Aunt Dictator."

* * *

While Mama and Daddy were out, Aunt Cecelia left Squirt in his high chair (when *I* baby-sit, I play with him; it's much more stimulating for him) and prepared a salad for lunch, and also began preparing dinner. Aunt Cecelia was so busy cooking that she hadn't gotten around to cleaning up Squirt yet.

"Aunt Di — I mean, Aunt Cecelia," I said, entering the kitchen, "Becca and I are going to take Squirt for a walk." (After I wash his face and hands, I thought.)

I was all dressed. And my hair was tidy. Aunt Cecelia wouldn't be able to find anything to complain about.

"Where are you going to take him?" she asked.

"Just up and down the street like we always do." I paused, then added, "I put him in his stroller and strap him in, and I never let him lean over and touch the wheels because he might get hurt."

Aunt Dictator looked outside. "Too cloudy," she announced.

I nearly exploded, but instead I said, "Okay. Then I'm going over to Mallory Pike's house."

"Who's Mallory?" my aunt asked.

"You met her once," I told her. "She's my best friend."

55

".Where does she live?"

"Nearby. I can ride my bike to her house."

"I don't think so." Aunt Dictator shook her head slowly. "No, I don't think so. I'm in charge now, and it looks like rain. The roads will get too slippery for bicycles."

That did it. I turned around and stomped out of the kitchen.

"Walk like a lady!" Aunt Cecelia called after me.

I didn't answer her. (But I did stop stomping.) Who did Aunt Cecelia think she was? Oh, yeah. My baby-sitter.

I ran upstairs to Becca's room. My poor sister had followed me to the kitchen before, but when she saw how unreasonable Aunt Cecelia was being, she had escaped back to her room. Becca is a little shy and very sensitive to criticism, so she wasn't about to face Aunt Cecelia until she thought the arguing was over.

"Becca," I said, "you can stop hiding out. I've got an idea. It's time to start our Aunt Cecelia project."

I whispered into Becca's ear, and she began to giggle. By the time Mama and Daddy returned, my sister and I had been hard at work. We had short-sheeted Aunt Dictator's bed. We'd filled one of her slippers with Daddy's shaving cream. We'd arranged a realistic rubber spider on her pillow and covered it with the bedspread.

Her room looked normal, but we knew better. Our only worry: Mama and Daddy couldn't see what we'd done, but when Aunt Dictator put on her slippers or got into bed, what would happen?

Would Mama and Daddy see how unfair our new sitter was? Would they give Aunt Cecelia a talking-to? Or would Becca and I just be in an awful lot of trouble?

Surprisingly, none of the above happened. At eleven o'clock that night, Aunt Cecelia was reading in bed. Mama stuck her head into the room to thank her for making her life so much easier. And all Aunt Cecelia said was, "You're welcome," even though she must have found the shaving cream and the spider. And she must have had to make her bed up again.

I did not know what to think of that.

CHAPTER 7

"Good-bye, Mama! Good luck!" I called.

"Have fun at work!" Becca added.

It was the next morning, and Mama and Daddy were leaving for their jobs together. I felt like I was sending Mama off to her first day of kindergarten.

My parents' cars rolled down the driveway. It was time for Becca and me to hustle or we'd be late for school.

"Take care of Squirt," Becca said seriously to Aunt Dictator, strapping her backpack on and picking up her lunch box.

"Yeah," I said. "Remember, he's allowed to watch *Sesame Street*, and he always needs an afternoon nap and usually a morning nap, too. And he likes to take a bottle of water to bed with him. Oh, and — "

Suddenly I stopped talking. Whoa. If looks could kill.

"Jessica," said my aunt crisply. "I raised children of my own."

You didn't raise Squirt, I thought.

I was not in a good mood by the time I left for school.

But when I came home that afternoon, I was in a much better frame of mind. I'd gotten an A- on a math test, I'd scored three baskets during gym, my creative-writing teacher had said he was impressed with the story I was working on, and I had a full (and Aunt Cecelia-free) afternoon ahead of me. I was supposed to baby-sit at the Rodowskys' and then go to the Monday BSC meeting.

I bounced through our front door. "Hello!" I called.

"SHHH!" was Aunt Cecelia's reply. "Your brother's asleep."

"*Now?*" I said. "He's usually awake by this time."

"Well, he isn't today."

Auntie Dictator, Auntie Dictator, Auntie Dictator, I sang to myself.

I put away my backpack, changed my clothes quickly, and dashed into the kitchen for a fast snack. I had to be at the Rodowskys' soon.

Aunt Cecelia was working at the stove when

I came in. I opened the refrigerator and surveyed the snack possibilities.

"Snack's on the table," said Aunt Cecelia, without turning around to look at me. (I think some adults actually *do* have eyes behind their heads. The eyes are just hidden by their hair, that's all.)

I looked at the table.

Milk and cookies. Kid stuff.

"I usually have a sandwich," I said, opening the fridge again.

"Not this close to dinner, you don't. You'll spoil your appetite."

"But I *do* get to eat a sandwich. Mama lets me. We eat lunch really early. Before it's even twelve o'clock."

"Two cookies," said Aunt Cecelia.

"I'll pass," I told her. "I'll eat at Jackie's house."

"Jackie? Who's Jackie? Not a boy, I hope."

"As a matter of fact, Jackie *is* a boy."

"Well, you are certainly not spending the afternoon with a *boy*."

"Aunt Cecelia, he's seven years old. I babysit for him."

My aunt was about to protest when Becca came home, as starving as I was. She also requested a sandwich and got two measly cookies instead. Since she ate hers, I ate mine after all. (Oh, I think I forgot to mention that the cookies weren't anything fun, like chocolate chip. They were oat-bran bars.)

"Okay," I said, jumping up from the table. "Gotta go! I'll be at the Rodowskys' until a little after five. Then I'll be at Claudia Kishi's for our Baby-sitters Club meeting."

"Wait a minute," said Aunt Cecelia. "*Where* are you going?"

"To the Rodowskys' and then to Claudia's."

"I don't know those people."

"But I do."

"But I can't let you go running off to strange places."

"They *aren't strange!*"

"They are to me."

"Aunt Cecelia, you don't understand. This sitting job is my responsibility. I baby-sit all the time. You have to let me go."

"I don't *have* to let you do anything," said Aunt Dictator. "Besides, *you* are *my* responsibility now. I'm in charge while your parents are out. If anything happens to you, I'm — "

"I know. You're responsible," I said. "But I have a commitment. I told the Rodowskys a week ago that I would baby-sit this afternoon. They're counting on me. And a good baby-sitter never lets her clients down. Unless there's an emergency," I added.

Aunt Cecelia looked thoughtful.

"You can call Mama or Daddy at work and tell them what my plans are. They'll say I can go. This is my schedule. And these are *my* responsibilities."

"All right," said Aunt Cecilia at last. "What time will you be home?"

"Ten after six. Baby-sitters Club meetings always end at six o'clock. Then I ride my bicycle home."

Aunt Cecelia nodded. "Very well, then."

I made a dash for the door — for two reasons. 1. I was about to be late. 2. I didn't want Aunt Dictator to change her mind.

I had to *speed* to the Rodowskys'. I was glad Aunt Cecelia couldn't see me. I didn't break any laws, but I nearly broke my head riding over a curb. I arrived at Jackie's house in one piece, though.

"Hi," I greeted Mrs. Rodowsky breathlessly. I glanced at my watch. "Boy, I just made it. I'm sorry I was almost late." (A good baby-sitter tries to get to any job, even the most routine one, a few minutes early in case the parents have special instructions, or there's a problem, such as a child who's going to cry a lot when Mommy leaves.)

"Don't worry, Jessi," said Mrs. R. as she let me inside. "I know I can count on you."

I wish Aunt Cecelia would count on me, I thought.

A few minutes later, Mrs. R. left with Shea. Archie was supposed to have gone with her — to be dropped off at soccer practice — but he had stayed at home that day, recovering from an ear infection.

"He's on the mend, though," his mother had told me. "He'll be back in school tomorrow. He doesn't need to stay in bed, and don't worry about medicine. I'll give him his next dose at suppertime."

So I was left with Jackie and Archie.

"Okay," I said enthusiastically to Jackie. "Let's get to work on your volcano. Did your mom and dad buy the things you need?"

"Yup," replied Jackie.

He and Archie and I were in the Rodowskys' playroom. Archie looked at his big brother and me with interest. "Can I help?" he asked.

"This is Jackie's project," I told Archie.

"Oh. Can I watch, then?"

"Sure," I replied. I turned to Jackie. "Now the first thing we need to do is build that box, the glass one with the wood frame that we'll put our volcano in," I said.

"*Our* volcano?" asked Jackie.

"I mean yours. Now let's see. Where are the instructions?"

"You don't have to worry about that," said Jackie. "My dad and I made a box over the weekend. It doesn't look exactly like the one in the picture, but it's glass, and it's big enough for the volcano."

"Oh, good," I said. I felt relieved. Building the box had sounded difficult, even harder than making a working volcano. "Then we can get started on the next step," I told Jackie.

"Yea! Papier-mâché!" he cried. (Just the *idea* of something messy is appealing to Jackie.)

"Nope," I said, referring to the instructions. "First we have to build up the layers of igneous, metamorphic, and sedimentary rock. We'll use the Plasticine for that. Did you buy three different colors of Plasticine?"

"What's Plasticine?" asked Archie, who was beginning to look bored.

"Modeling clay," I told him. "Did you get some, Jackie?"

"Yup. We got red, yellow, and brown. But, Jessi, *clay* doesn't look like rocks." Jackie sounded worried.

"It doesn't matter," I told him. "It's supposed to *represent* rocks."

"Can't we just build a volcano?" he asked.

"Not if you want to win a prize in the fair. You have to do a really terrific project. Now where's the clay? And the box?"

Jackie set out the materials on an old table in the playroom. He watched while I built up the layers of rock that lie under volcanoes. It didn't take me too long.

"Goody!" he exclaimed as soon as I was done. "Papier-mâché time!"

Before I knew it, Jackie was mixing flour and water, and Archie was tearing strips of newspaper. Apparently, they had made papier-mâché before.

"Goop, goop, goop," sang Jackie, as he slurped his hands in and out of the pasty bowl. "Hey, this is a good batch, Archie," he said. Jackie was up to his elbows in goo. He grinned happily.

"Okay," I instructed, "take the papier-mâché and build a mountain on top of the clay, and around this tin can. Don't fill the can in. That's where we'll put the chemicals to make the lava."

"Mmmm," said Jackie. He held up his hands and let the goop drip back into the bowl. Then he got an itch and wiped his cheek, leaving papier-mâché smeared across it.

I tried to ignore that. I read up on igneous, metamorphic, and sedimentary rocks. But in the background, I was aware of cries of, "Got you! I'm the slime monster!" and, "Hey, Archie, look. If you wrap the papier-mâché around your arm you can make a cast," and, "Cool. Wrap me *all* up, Jackie. Make me a mummy!"

I glanced at the boys. They were having the time of their lives. Papier-mâché was everywhere — except surrounding the can in the glass box. Jackie hadn't started his mountain yet.

"This is so, so fun!" he exclaimed, just as I was about to tell him to get to work. "I can't wait to see lava, lava everywhere!"

I looked at my watch. "Time to clean up, guys," I said. "Your mom and Shea will be home soon."

"You know what, Jessi?" Jackie replied. "This was the best afternoon of my life!"

CHAPTER 8

Thursday

Another afternoon with David Michael and Emily Michelle. Nannie was practicing with her bowling team. I'm glad she gets out in the afternoons, because her mornings are spent entirely with Emily. Anyway, it was a pretty quiet afternoon, but even so, something intresting happened:

Jackie and Margo now have one more competitor in the science fair. I'd never have guessed it, but David Michael wants to enter, so I tried to help him choose a project and work with Emily on naming the parts of her body at the same time. It was a challenging and fun afternoon. I'm still thinking of becoming a teacher some day.

Uh-oh. I should have known.

Competition.

When Kristy gets involved in something, the competition heats up right away. (I bet if you opened Webster's and looked up "competition," you'd find a picture of Kristy's face.)

Kristy now saw the science fair as a competition among Mallory, herself, and me, as well as among all the kids in the fair. It would be like . . . well, like if David Michael won, Kristy would have won. In other words, she would have beaten me. At least that's what I thought at first. Things turned out quite differently.

Anyway, Kristy was baby-sitting that afternoon. Nannie had just driven off in her car, the Pink Clinker, and Kristy was trying to think of something fun to do with her little brother and sister. Usually, David Michael wants to play outside, but that afternoon he curled himself up in an armchair with his second-grade science book and began poring over it.

"What are you doing?" asked Kristy. (David Michael practically has to be bolted to his desk to do the small amount of homework he sometimes gets. He's smart, but he doesn't like school much, and he *really* doesn't like homework, particularly during softball season.)

"Well," said David Michael, "see, there's going to be this science fair at school. Do you know what that is?"

Kristy hid a smile. Of course she knew what it was. She'd gone to Stoneybrook Elementary herself and had entered several of the fairs. But all she said was, "Yes."

"So I might enter it," said David Michael casually.

"Oh, yeah?" Kristy replied, just as casually.

"Yeah. There are prizes."

David Michael continued to flip through the book, while Kristy kept an eye on Emily, who was stacking blocks nearby.

"But," David Michael went on, "I'm not too good in science."

"You could enter anyway," Kristy told him. "Science isn't my best subject, either, but it's fun to enter the fair. Is there anything about science that you like?"

"Space," said David Michael immediately. "Aliens. Flying saucers."

"Some people say that's science *fiction*," Kristy told him. "You know. Made-up stuff."

"Well, I still like to think about Mars and Pluto and all the planets. I like Saturn best, because of its rings."

"So do a project on the solar system," said Kristy.

"Make a list of all our planets?" suggested David Michael.

"No. Something a little more ambitious. Go out there and show what you can *really* do. Like when you're up at bat in a softball game. Think, 'I can do something big.' "

"I'll make a huge Saturn!" cried David Michael, inspired. "I'll use a beach ball, and I'll put hula hoops around it for rings."

"That's the spirit," said Kristy, "but it isn't science-y enough. You're going to be competing against some kids who are playing hardball."

"Huh?"

"Kids who really know science. Kids who will do great experiments. You've got to do something better than them if you want to win."

"Help me, Kristy," said her brother, plaintively.

Kristy paused. "I'll *help* you," she said at last, "but I won't do the project for you. Just like I can give you pointers on how to pitch a ball, but when you're on the pitcher's mound during a game, *you've* got to throw the ball, not me. Okay?"

"Okay." David Michael turned back to his book.

"Hey, Emily," Kristy said, "what are you building?"

Emily looked up from a messy tower she was working on. "Building," she repeated, smiling.

"You're building a building?"

Emily looked frustrated. "No!"

"*What* are you building?" Kristy repeated patiently.

"Bwocks."

Kristy sighed. Emily Michelle is what the pediatrician calls "language delayed." And it's no wonder. The first part of her short life was spent in an orphanage in Vietnam, where she was spoken to in a foreign language (Vietnamese, of course), when she was spoken to at all. Then she was uprooted at the age of two and flown to a completely new country where she didn't understand a word anyone said to her. Believe it or not, *Claudia* has been working with Emily some afternoons, teaching her vocabulary and concepts and other things that most two-year-olds already know.

Emily looked frustrated with her block-building, so Kristy decided to give her something new to do.

"Hey, Emily," she said. She led her away from the blocks. "Show me your *nose*. Where is your *nose?*"

"Nose," said Emily, pointing to it proudly.

"Good girl!" cried Kristy. (Claudia said that Emily learned fastest when she was praised for her good work.)

Then, without being asked, Emily pointed to her eye and said triumphantly, "Eye!"

"Great!" exclaimed Kristy. "Where's your ear?"

Emily pointed. "Ear."

"Oh! I just thought of a great song for you, Miss Emily," said Kristy suddenly. "Come over here. We need space."

Kristy led Emily to the middle of the den, away from furniture. "Watch this," she said, and sang a song she'd learned in preschool.

Head, shoulders, knees and toes, knees and toes.
Head, shoulders, knees and toes, knees and toes.
Eyes and ears and nose and mouth and chin.
Head, shoulders, knees and toes!

Kristy pointed to each body part as she sang the word. The song is fun, especially when you get going fast. (I can't wait until Squirt is old enough for it.)

Emily had smiled while she watched Kristy.

Now Kristy took her sister's hands and placed them on her head and shoulders and so forth as she sang the song again. Emily laughed.

Kristy and her sister were going through the song for the fourth time when David Michael cried, "I've got it!"

"What?" asked Kristy.

"I'll draw a picture of each planet in our solar system. I'll color them in really carefully and I'll write their names by them."

"We-ell," said Kristy. "Are you giving this your best shot?"

"Guess not," replied David Michael. "Hey! How about, like, I get all my space monsters and all my astronauts and show them having a big, big, fight . . . on Venus?"

Kristy hesitated.

"I know, I know. Not good enough," said David Michael.

An hour went by. David Michael suggested several more ideas to Kristy, who kept encouraging him to go one step further. Kristy and Emily sang their new song together.

It was just before Kristy's mom and Watson came home from work that David Michael jumped up from his chair and announced, "This time I really *do* have a great idea!"

"What?" asked Kristy, who was losing hope.

"I'll build a mobile and it will show all the planets. I mean, I'll hang them in the right order: Mercury, Venus, Earth, Mars. You know. And I'll put the sun in the center. Maybe I'll even make moons. At least, I'll make *our* moon."

"Now *that*," said Kristy, "sounds like a good idea. You'd really be showing something. Maybe you could even fix up the mobile so the planets could turn around each other."

"Maybe . . ." said David Michael uncertainly. But Kristy said he acted pretty excited when his mom and Watson came home. He told them all about the science fair and his solar system mobile.

Then Emily had to show off, too. "Eyes and ears and nose and mouf and shin," she sang happily. Kristy couldn't get her to sing the rest of the song, but it didn't matter. David Michael was already clamoring for Kristy's help with his project.

Kristy and David Michael were now official competition in the science fair.

CHAPTER 9

Friday

I've always heard of playing music to plants, but I've never seen it done -- until today. I was baby-sitting for Charlotte Johanssen, and she was working on her project for the Stoneybrook Elementary science fair. Okay, you guys, I know that some of you are helping kids get ready for the fair. Well, now I am, too. And I don't want to brag or anything, but you know how smart Charlotte is. She's a year ahead of herself in school. Anyway, I gave her a couple of suggestions for her experiment (she is conducting an actual experiment) and she caught on right away. Her work was interrupted when Becca Ramsey came over, though. Poor Becca. I feel bad for her. You too, Jessi.

When Stacey arrived at the Johanssens' on Friday afternoon, Charlotte didn't run for the door as she usually does when she knows Stacey's going to be her sitter. Instead, Dr. Johanssen answered the bell.

"Hi, Stacey," she said. "How are you feeling?" (Dr. Johanssen knows about Stacey's diabetes and has been a help sometimes, even though she isn't Stacey's doctor.)

"Still kind of funny these days," Stacey admitted. "I'll probably see my doctor in New York soon."

"Well, that's good. Remember, you can always call me if you or your mom have any questions."

"Thanks," replied Stacey gratefully.

Dr. Johanssen led Stacey into the kitchen. "Charlotte is as busy as a bee in here," she said. "I'll let Char tell you what she's doing, but I've got to get to the clinic now. You know where the emergency numbers are. Mr. Johanssen will be home early today — around five o'clock or five-fifteen. You'll have plenty of time to get to your club meeting this afternoon."

"Okay," said Stacey. "Thanks. See you!"

"See you," Charlotte echoed absently, not looking up from her work.

Dr. Johanssen smiled, shook her head, and left.

"What are you doing, Char?" asked Stacey. "What's your project?"

"It's not a project. It's an experiment."

Charlotte is just eight years old, but she's very bright. She's an excellent reader and does extremely well in school.

"An actual experiment?" said Stacey. "You mean you're going to discover something?"

"I hope so."

"Tell me what you're doing."

"Okay," said Charlotte eagerly.

In front of her were three jelly jars. They had been cleaned thoroughly. In the bottom of each jar was some damp, white stuff.

"Well," said Charlotte, "my experiment will show if music helps plants grow better, or if some *kinds* of music help plants grow better."

"What's that white stuff?" asked Stacey, pointing to the bottoms of the jars.

"Wet cotton balls," Charlotte told her. "Can you believe it? If you bury seeds in damp cotton, they'll start growing faster than if you put them in regular dirt. So I put three lima bean seeds in each jar. The seeds are just beginning to sprout. I keep the jars on this windowsill here in the kitchen. They all get sunlight part of the day. And I water them the same amount each day. *But*, here's the difference. Every afternoon, I take this jar, Jar Number One, upstairs to my room and play classical music to it for half an hour. I close the door so the other plants can't hear the music. Then, I bring Jar Number One downstairs, and take Jar Number Two upstairs. I play rock-and-roll music to those beans. I play it at exactly the same volume I played the classical music."

"What about Jar Number Three?" asked Stacey, already impressed with what Charlotte was doing.

"Oh, I don't play any music to that one. Because maybe music *isn't* good for plants. After all, plants that grow wild don't hear music."

"And I guess you're keeping track of how the plants grow and stuff like that," said Stacey.

"What?"

"Well, you're charting them or something, aren't you?"

"No. I mean, look at them. You can see for yourself. The sprouts in Jar Number One are bigger than in the other two jars. Those are the sprouts that hear classical music. I bet they're going to be tallest."

"But what if they were tallest, but the plants that heard the rock-and-roll music grew thicker than the others? Or their leaves were brighter or something?"

Stacey was going to keep on talking, but Charlotte got the message right away. "Oh, wow!" she exclaimed. "I've got to keep all kinds of records and stuff, don't I? I should make charts and graphs. I should measure the plants every day." She giggled. "I could keep a growth chart for them just like Mommy and Daddy kept for me when I was little. And I could make a chart showing their coloring and — and what else did you say, Stacey?"

"The thickness of the plants."

"Oh, yeah. Boy, I've got a lot of work to do."

Charlotte assembled crayons, a pencil, a ruler, graph paper, and plain white paper on the kitchen table. Stacey sat down next to her to watch her work. But before Charlotte began, she jumped up, exclaiming, "Oops! I forgot! I've got to take Jar Number One upstairs. It needs its music."

Charlotte carried the jar up the stairs, and soon Stacey could hear a few strains of what she thought was some music by Vivaldi. (Mrs. McGill loves Vivaldi.) Then Charlotte must have closed her door, because the music dissolved into silence.

For awhile after that, Stacey and Charlotte

sat at the kitchen table. Char worked hard, occasionally asking Stacey for suggestions or help. Then, after awhile, Charlotte glanced up, looking like the timid child she used to be.

"Stacey?"

"Yeah, Char?"

"Do you think that maybe — I mean, if you have time — you could come to the science fair? Only if you want to. It's just a kids' thing. I know that. And you're thirteen, but — "

"Charlotte, you know I'll be there. If you want me there, I'll come. Even if you hadn't invited me, I probably would have come, anyway. You're like my sister. I'm interested in everything you do."

"Thank you, Stacey!" exclaimed Charlotte, jumping up to give her a hug.

Charlotte settled down to work again, and Stacey admitted to me later that she couldn't help thinking that Char's project for the science fair was the best one she'd heard of so far. It was a real experiment. Although if Jackie's volcano really did erupt, that *would* be pretty exciting.

A few moments later, the doorbell rang.

"Do you want me to get it?" asked Stacey.

"Please," said Charlotte. "A half an hour's up, and I've got to switch jars and music right now."

So Stacey answered the door. Guess who was standing on the stoop. Becca — my own sister and Charlotte's best friend.

"Come on in," said Stacey.

Becca stepped inside, looking glum.

"What's wrong?" Stacey asked.

"Everything," mumbled Becca. "Where's Charlotte?"

"Upstairs. She'll be right down, though. She's working on her project for the science fair."

"Oh, yeah. The plants."

Charlotte trotted downstairs then. "Hi," she said. "Well, Jar Number Two is listening to Duran Duran." She paused. "Becca? What's the matter?"

"Oh, it's Aunt Dictator," said Becca, flopping into a chair in the living room.

Char and Stacey couldn't help giggling. *Aunt Dictator?*

"Yeah. That's what Jessi calls Aunt Cecelia."

"What's your aunt doing?" asked Charlotte.

"What *isn't* she doing!" Becca countered. "You know, Aunt Cecelia is supposed to be a baby-sitter, but she sure could take some lessons. She isn't like you guys at all," she said to Stacey. (Stacey guessed that "you guys" meant the members of the BSC.) "She never listens to Jessi and me; she just orders us around. And she doesn't believe us. She doesn't trust us, either. It was like when I got stranded on the island with Dawn and everyone the weekend Mama and Daddy left Jessi in charge. When Jessi called Aunt Cecelia to tell her about the emergency, Aunt Cecelia raced to Stoneybrook and took charge like Jessi didn't even exist.

"And," Becca went on, "she *thinks* she's so great with Squirt, but she isn't. She leaves him in his playpen when he should be walking around exploring things, or playing with me.

"You know what else is weird? Jessi and I have been playing all these practical jokes on Aunt Dictator, and she hasn't said a *word* about them."

"What kinds of jokes?" Charlotte wanted to know.

Becca explained, and Charlotte giggled helplessly.

"We figure," said Becca, "that if we do enough awful things, Aunt Cecelia will get fed up and leave."

"You mean, make like a *tree* and *leave?*" said Charlotte.

The sillies were setting in, Stacey could tell. But she let the girls go ahead and plot Aunt Cecelia's demise. She didn't think Becca would carry out any of their ideas, and she thought

82

that taking imaginary action might make Becca feel better.

The girls discussed: tying Aunt Cecelia to a chair and telling the Ramseys that robbers had done it; hiding Aunt Cecelia's hair combs, so that she couldn't look perfect one morning; dressing up as Avon ladies and selling Aunt Cecelia jars full of water; coloring Squirt's beautiful curls with wash-out green dye; and other things bound to drive poor Aunt Cecelia crazy.

Stacey laughed along with the girls, but she was worried. There are serious problems in the Ramsey household, she thought.

CHAPTER 10

"I wonder what the world's record for a gum chain is," said Mal thoughtfully as she and I worked dutifully at ours.

"I don't know," I replied. "Maybe we could look it up in the Guinness book under 'Gum Chain, Longest.' "

It was a Wednesday afternoon. Mal and I were in Claudia's room, waiting for a BSC meeting to begin.

"Claud?" I asked. "Do you have the Guinness book here?"

"Yes, but I don't know where it is," she replied. She was separating the contents of a package of Neccos, pushing all the violet-colored ones aside. Claud doesn't like purple Neccos.

"Oh," said Mal. "Well, I'll look it up at home. You know, if by some chance our gum chain beats the record, then I think we should try to braid the world's longest friendship bracelet next."

"But what would be the point?" I asked. "No one could wear it."

"So what? No one can eat a five hundred-pound pancake, but people are always making things like that, trying to set records."

"I know," I replied, "but five hundred people could each eat a *piece* of the pancake," I pointed out.

"Would you want to eat something that four hundred and ninety-nine other people were touching? And that had probably been buttered by an army of people skating across it with slabs of butter strapped to the bottoms of their shoes?"

"You guys! Cut it out!" exclaimed Mary Anne, looking absolutely green as she entered club headquarters and heard that last comment.

"Yeah, Mal. What's gotten into you?" I asked. "You'd think Aunt Dictator lived at *your* house."

"Nothing. I'm just pointing out to you guys that — "

"Order! Order! It is now five-thirty," Kristy interrupted.

I looked around. The seven of us were assembled in our usual places. Since it was a Wednesday, Stacey didn't have to collect dues.

"Any club business?" asked Kristy, as she always does.

"Logan baby-sat for the Arnold twins and Marilyn accidentally locked herself in the basement," said Mary Anne. "Logan had to rescue her through the outside cellar door."

We giggled.

"I know it sounds funny," Mary Anne continued, "but we should remember how that basement door works."

"Right," agreed Kristy. "Everybody, make a mental note of that."

(Claudia pretended to write something across her forehead.)

The phone rang then and Dawn answered it. "Hi, Mrs. Perkins. . . . A week from Saturday? I'll have Mary Anne check, and I'll call you right back."

Dawn hung up the phone. "The Perkinses have a big, fancy party to go to. They need someone to baby-sit a week from Saturday," she told Mary Anne. "It'll be a late night."

Mary Anne was already looking through the record book. "Hmmm," she said. "Believe it or not, we're all busy. We'll have to call Logan or Shannon. I'll take care of it."

In the end, Kristy's friend Shannon wound up with the job for the Perkinses. Then the BSC members waited for the phone to ring again. It didn't. So we began to talk.

"You guys should see Margo's shadow box for the science fair," said Mal. "I want her to win, and I'm helping her when she asks for help, but mostly she's working on her own. I don't know what kind of research she's doing, but she seems to have decided that Barbie, Ken, and Skipper inhabit the moon, and that they dress in pink and silver sparkly outfits, kind of like the ones that the Jetsons used to wear. You know, on that old cartoon show?"

"Yes," said several of us, laughing.

"So then I asked Margo what people on the moon would eat, and she said, 'Well, I guess they couldn't grow any food in moon dust. They'd have to bring food with them like the astronauts did.' So she put Tang and little plastic pastries and eggs and things from her dollhouse into the shadow box. To be honest," Mal finished up, "the shadow box looks like a Barbie scene with a picture of the earth in the background."

"Why don't you correct her?" I asked. "Help her start over. Give her some books to read. Make her do it right."

"Nope. That's not what I'm there for," said Mal. "As her sister *or* her baby-sitter. This is her project. She's got to learn for herself."

"Well, she won't win," spoke up Kristy. She paused. "But then, David Michael isn't going to win, either. He's making a model of the planets in the solar system, remember? I told you guys about that."

We nodded.

"He happened to choose a very tough project. It's difficult to set up the planets so that they're at different distances from the sun. Right now, he's got them all going around the sun in one big circle — Mercury followed by Venus followed by Earth, and so on. I tried to show him a way to get the distances right, but he doesn't understand what I mean and he won't let me do it for him. I don't blame him. I'm the most competitive person here — I think — "

(Claudia snorted.)

"But I'm not going to do his project for him. That's his job and we both know it. This is like the Little Miss Stoneybrook Pageant, in a way." (The pageant Kristy was referring to had been held in Stoneybrook awhile back. A whole bunch of the kids we sit for wanted to enter. We could train them and coach them and rehearse them all we wanted, but when it got down to the big day, the kids were on their own.) "David Michael has to work his project out himself."

"How come?" I asked. "We rehearsed the girls for the pageant."

"That was different," said Mal. "We *rehearsed* them, but we couldn't get up on stage for them."

That was when I began to see that my friends and I weren't going to be as competitive as I'd first thought.

"Stacey," I said, after we'd taken a couple of job calls, "aren't you giving Charlotte a lot of help with *her* project?"

"Not really. I suggested that she needed some — what do you call it? — some data, to show the results of her experiment. I didn't say much more than that and Charlotte was off and running, making graphs, keeping charts."

Hmm, I thought.

"How's Jackie's volcano coming along?" Dawn asked me.

"Terrific!" I said. "I hate to say this, but I think Jackie's project is going to be the best one at the fair." (I couldn't help bragging.) "I think it'll win first place. His volcano isn't just going to explode, it's going to show the makeup of a volcano. You know, the kinds of rocks a volcano sits on, all that stuff."

"And Jackie did this research by himself?" asked Mal incredulously.

"Well, no. I found the books for him. And I told him about igneous, metamorphic, and sedimentary rocks. And I'm helping him build the volcano around a tin can."

There was a silence in club headquarters.

Finally, Mary Anne said, "Jessi, it sounds like you're doing Jackie's project *for* him. . . . Not to be rude or anything."

"No, I'm not!" I exclaimed. "I'm not doing it for him. He's right there when I read about volcanoes or when I work on his project. He knows what's going on." I stopped talking. I listened to what I'd just said. *Was* I doing Jackie's project for him? Nah. I just wanted to give him a lot of help so he could win for once in his life.

"You're sure you're not taking over?" asked Mal. "Maybe by accident?"

"No way! Of course not. But I'll tell you who *is* taking over. Aunt Cecelia. She won't let Becca or me do *any*thing on our own. It's rules, rules, rules. Plus, she lays out our clothes for us each night. She practically cuts our meat for us. Becca and I know she doesn't trust us. I mean, not like she thinks we'd steal or anything. It's just that she doesn't believe we're capable of doing things that an eleven-year-old and an eight-year-old *are* capable of.

"If she were a good baby-sitter, she'd trust us. Our *parents* trust us. I mean, they set limits, but they do trust us. They let me use the stove and cook. They let us choose our own clothes. Not necessarily in stores, but once we have the clothes they let us decide what to wear to school or to a restaurant or wherever we're going. Aunt Cecelia doesn't trust us to do *any*thing right."

"Jessi, have you and Becca spoken to your parents about Aunt Cecelia?" asked Mary Anne. "Do they know how you feel?"

I sighed. "No. I mean, no, we haven't spoken to them, and no, they don't know how we feel."

"Why not?" asked Kristy sensibly.

"Because Mama and Daddy are so pleased to have Aunt Cecelia here. It solves all sorts of problems for them now that Mama's working. Plus, they think they're making Aunt Cecelia happy. She's been so lonely since her husband died."

"But, Jessi," said Stacey, "Becca told me

what you and she are doing to your aunt. Don't you think that talking to your parents would be a little nicer than playing tricks on her?"

I could feel my face flush, especially as I explained to the other club members about the tricks. Then I added, "And that's another thing. Becca and I feel like we can't talk to Mama and Daddy *because* of the tricks. For some reason Aunt Dictator hasn't mentioned the tricks to our parents. It's like they never happened. Becca and I are afraid that if we confront Mama and Daddy, Aunt Cecelia will tell on us. I'm completely stuck. I don't know what to do. And I *want* to talk to my parents, particularly because Aunt Cecelia really isn't a very good baby-sitter. She's not too playful with Squirt. She does things for him that he should be learning to do for himself, and, I don't know, it's a big mess."

I felt miserable. I know I looked miserable. This was because Dawn said, "You look miserable, Jessi."

"Boy," I replied. "If I have kids of my own, I'm *never* going to treat them the way Aunt Dictator treats Becca and Squirt and me."

"Famous last words," said Kristy, laughing.

There was a pause, then we took some

phone calls, and then, out of the blue, Mal said, "You know the five hundred-pound pan-cake? I wonder how they ever mixed the batter for it. In a cement-mixer?"

We left the meeting laughing.

CHAPTER 11

"Phoo! Phoo! Phee-*ew!* Jessi, when this volcano erupts, it is going to be the biggest mess." Jackie looked thrilled at the prospect.

There were just two days left until the science fair. The volcano had been built. The can inside it was filled with the chemicals, which we had been able to find, although Jackie and his mom had had to go to four different places before they found them.

"Jessi?" asked Jackie. I was sitting for him on another afternoon.

"Yeah?"

"Shouldn't we try the volcano just once? I mean, what if it doesn't work when the judges come around at the science fair?"

Although Jackie had a point, I had to tell him, "No. We can only let the volcano erupt once. Otherwise, you'll take a messy, gooey project to the fair. It won't be as impressive as if it erupts for the first time. Maybe we *should* test the chemicals, though. We could put them in another can, light them — *I* have to light the match, by the way — and make sure they really form the ash that's supposed to pour out of the crater. We'll test it on your driveway and then wash the mess away with the garden hose."

"All *right!*" cried Jackie. "Oh, boy. A mess!"

Jackie and I carried the chemicals, an empty coffee can, and a packet of matches out to his driveway. We followed the instructions for putting the chemicals in the can.

Then I said, "Okay, I'm going to toss a match in the can. By the way, Jackie, an adult will have to do that for you at the science fair, too. Me, your mom or dad, or one of the judges. Okay?"

"Okay."

"Now get ready. Stand back!"

Jackie ran to the edge of the driveway. I lit a match, tossed it in the can, and ran. I turned around just in time to see ash spewing from the can and running down the sides. It was very realistic.

"Awesome!" exclaimed Jackie.

"It worked!" I cried.

Jackie ran to the can, but I stopped him. "Don't touch anything! The chemicals might burn your hands."

We turned on the hose, cleaned out the can, and sprayed the ash down the driveway and into a sewer.

"Now," I said to Jackie, "it is time to begin final preparation of your project."

"Final preparation?" squeaked Jackie. "I thought we were done."

"Oh, no," I told him as we walked back into the house. "We have to figure out how you're going to present your project. It needs a name. And you have to be able to tell the judges about it, not just have someone toss the match in and let the volcano erupt. How are you going to demonstrate your project?"

"Well," said Jackie, sounding sort of mixed up, "I'm not sure."

"All right. First, let's make a sign to label your volcano. What do you want to call your project?"

"I want to call it 'My Volcano,' " said Jackie.

I shook my head.

"*The* volcano? *A* volcano?"

"No, no, no. It has to be much catchier," I told him.

We stood over the volcano in its glass box. "How about 'Welcome to the World of Volcanic Activity'?" I suggested proudly.

"Okay," agreed Jackie.

"You make the sign to hang in front of the

96

volcano," I said. I handed Jackie a piece of paper and a Magic Marker.

Jackie worked laboriously for fifteen minutes. Then he proudly held up a sign that looked like this:

Wellcom to the Wurld of
Vulcanice Acitivtie

"Jackie! No!" I exclaimed. "You've at least got to spell things right. You can't hang up a sign like that."

"But these are hard words. You have to help me."

"After all the studying we've done, you should know how to spell 'volcanic' and 'activity,' " I said. "Here, *I'll* make the sign."

Jackie stared at the ground. And I thought, Boy, I have to do *all* the work. I even have to make the sign.

This is what I made:

Welcome to the World of
Volcanic Activity

"There. Now *that's* a sign," I told Jackie. I set it near his project. "What do you think of it?"

"Nice," he mumbled.

"Now, on to the next thing," I said enthusiastically.

"What next thing?" cried Jackie.

"We're heading over to Stoneybrook Elementary to see where the science fair will be held. We've got to stake out the best spot for your project. Mal told me the judges walk around the all-purpose room in a circle, starting at the front. I think your project should be one of the last they see. That way, they'll remember it when they're judging. Plus, they'll be really impressed after all the goofy stuff they've looked at, like Barbie dolls on the moon."

Jackie didn't even ask what I was talking about. He just put on the sweater I handed him and followed me out the back door and along the streets to the school.

"I hope the teachers are getting the room ready for the fair," I said as we neared Stoneybrook Elementary.

"They are," said Jackie. "The room was closed today."

"Good," I replied.

Jackie led me around to the back of the

school, and we peered through the windows of the all-purpose room.

"There're Mr. Peterson and Ms. Handy. They're the janitors," said Jackie. "It looks like they're putting desks in a big circle."

"I see a banner," I pointed out. "Look over the stage. Pretty nice, huh?"

Stretched from one end of the room to the other was a long paper banner that read: STON-EYBROOK ELEMENTARY SCHOOL SCIENCE FAIR.

Jackie began to look excited. "And they're putting up pictures of dinosaurs and planets and birds and — and *every*thing on the walls!"

"Yeah!" I agreed. "Now let's see. What would be the best desk for you?" I looked and looked and finally decided on one. "That desk. Over there," I said, pointing. "It must be at the end of the judges' rounds. We've got to get here early, Jackie, so you can set up your project on that desk."

Jackie nodded distractedly, still looking in awe at the decorations. "The fair is a big deal, isn't it?" he said. "I never went to it before."

"It sure is a big deal. Think how you'll feel when you win. I wonder what your prize will be?"

"I don't care," said Jackie. "I just want to have the best project here. Then I can show Ian and John and Danny and all those mean guys in my class that I can do something really good. I bet *they* never built a volcano."

"Probably not," I agreed.

We began to walk home. "Okay," I said. "Last thing. You've got two days to memorize what you're going to tell the judges about your project."

Jackie straightened his shoulders. "I'm going to say, 'This is my volcano. I built it myself. You light the chemicals and the ash goes *phoo, phoo, PHEW* out of the can!' "

"Oh, no, you're not. Jackie, this is a *science* fair. You've got to explain how a volcano works. Remember the kinds of rocks we built our volcano on? Remember their names?"

"Iggus, morphus, and sedentary?"

I sighed. "Almost. Ig*neo*us, *me*tamorph*ic*, and sed*imen*tary."

Jackie repeated the words fairly well.

"Okay, now what you want to say is that igneous rocks are born from fire, the molten rock that lies several miles below the surface of our earth. Above them are metamorphic rocks that have been changed by the heat . . ."

I finished my speech before we reached the Rodowskys'. I made Jackie start to memorize it. He wasn't bad. He stumbled on words a few times but he learned quickly.

When we'd been home for about twenty minutes, Jackie could spout off, "Igneous rocks are born from fire, the molten rock that lies several miles below the surface of the earth."

Awhile later, the speech was memorized.

"All right, hand signals."

"*Hand* signals?!"

"Yes."

"You mean like when I'm on my bike and I'm turning left and I stick out my left hand?"

"No. I guess I meant to say 'hand *gestures.*' "

"To impress the judges?"

Like I said, Jackie is a fast learner. "You got it," I told him. "See, I think you should even have a pointer. When you say, 'igneous rocks,' point to the bottom layer of Plasticine. When you say, 'metamorphic rocks,' point to the next layer, and so forth. Also, just as the chemicals are about to be lit — throw your hands in the air and say, 'the miracle of a volcano comes to life before our very eyes.' *Then* give your speech."

Jackie was grinning. He was going to get to put on a show.

"This'll be fun," he said, showing almost as much enthusiasm as when we'd set off the volcano on the driveway.

When Mrs. Rodowsky, Archie, and Shea came home, Jackie gleefully demonstrated his entire project — pointers, hand gestures, and all. I was late leaving for home, but I didn't mind. I was glad to see Jackie so happy.

CHAPTER 12

I might not have minded that I left the Rodowskys' a little late, but Aunt Dictator sure did. She met me at our front door. I mean, she was just standing there waiting for me, arms crossed, mouth grim.

"You're late," she said.

(I was ten minutes late.) "I know, I'm sorry. Jackie was so excited about his volcano that I wanted — "

"When I am in charge," Aunt Cecelia interrupted me (When isn't she in charge? I wondered), "you follow my rules. You are responsible to me. You must call me if you are going to be late. Is that understood? *You must be responsible.* And part of being responsible is letting people know where you are."

Sheesh, I thought. If I'd known I was going to be half an *hour* late, of course I would have called. But *ten minutes?* Mama and Daddy don't worry if I'm ten minutes late. They don't stand at doors with mental stopwatches going.

Aunt Cecelia had closed the door behind me and we were facing each other in the foyer.

"Take off your coat," said Aunt Cecelia.

Obediently, I took it off.

"Aunt — Aunt Cecelia," I said. ("Aunt Dictator" had almost slipped out. I wondered if that would ever *really* happen.) "Mama and Daddy are strict with Becca and me. Squirt, too. But they're not . . . um . . ." (I almost said "not unreasonable") "I mean, they only get worried when they really need to. They wouldn't worry about ten minutes."

"Jessica, I am in charge. Late is late, whether it's two minutes, two hours, or two days." (That "two days" thing was a low blow. She was referring to Becca getting stranded on the island, which she still claimed was my fault.)

"But honestly, Aunt Cecelia, Mama and Daddy really don't care about ten minutes. If I knew I was going to be much later, I would have called. I always do. Once I called, and Mama said, 'Oh, Jessi. Thank you for letting us know — but we weren't even worried yet!' See, the rules here are that if — "

"I don't know how many times I have to tell you about the rules here, young lady. They are mine when I'm in charge. Period."

"Okay, okay, okay."

"Jessica! No backtalk."

"That wasn't backtalk!"

"It sounded like it."

"Well, it wasn't." I looked at my watch. "Uh-oh!" I grabbed my jacket back out of the closet. "I have to leave. I'm going to be late for the BSC meeting."

"*Oh*, no," said Aunt Cecelia. "You're not going to any meeting. Not today. Not after what you did."

"Because I was ten minutes late?!" I exclaimed. I couldn't believe it.

"Yes. Because you were late and you didn't call me. You were irresponsible."

"Aunt Cecelia, don't you trust me? I'm not irresponsible. I can do things for myself. And I do the *right* things. If I were irresponsible I wouldn't have gone to Jackie's to baby-sit today. And missing a club meeting is very irresponsible. The other girls count on me. We all count on each other. We don't miss meetings unless we're sick or there's an emergency or something like a dance rehearsal comes up. When that happens, I let my friends know ahead of time. I can't just not go."

"Yes, you can. You're being punished. And if you carry this much further, you won't be able to attend Friday's meeting, either."

My mouth hung open. I just stood there,

gazing at my aunt's angry face. Slowly the rest of the room came into focus — the clock on the chest, the open closet door, the boots on the floor of the closet, the striped wallpaper, and, standing in the doorway to the kitchen, Becca and Squirt. They were taking the scene in, and both looked frightened. Squirt was clinging to Becca's hand.

I think it was the sight of their scared faces that prompted me to do what I did next — defy Aunt Cecelia.

"You're not *really* in charge," I told her. "Maybe you're the sitter, but Mama and Daddy are in charge of our house, and I am going to call them. If they say I can go to the meeting, then I can go. . . . And you can't stop me from calling," I added, dashing into the kitchen.

I reached the phone before Aunt Dictator could even open her mouth. First I called Daddy.

"Mr. Ramsey's office," said his secretary.

"Oh, hi, Ed," I said, trying not to sound shaky or upset. "This is Jessi. Can I speak to my dad, please?"

"He's out of the office, Jess," Ed replied. (Ed is one of the few people who calls me Jess. I kind of like it.) "Is this an emergency?"

I hesitated. "No," I said at last. Emergencies

are fires and accidents and injuries. I wanted to talk to Daddy badly, but this was not an emergency and I didn't want to do anything *irresponsible*.

"Do you want me to tell your father you called?" asked Ed.

"That's okay. I'll see him at home tonight," I replied.

"Okay."

Ed and I hung up.

I glanced over my shoulder at Aunt Cecelia, who was watching me carefully. I turned around, picked up the phone again, and started to dial Mama's new work number. But halfway through, I quit. Mama had said that, until she was used to her job, Becca and I shouldn't call her at the office — unless there was an emergency and we couldn't get hold of Daddy.

Okay. No emergency, no call to Mama.

I hung up, defeated. Have you ever heard the saying, "Someone's got you over a barrel"? Well, Aunt Cecelia had me over a barrel. It meant that she'd put me in a situation I couldn't get out of. I had no options. In this case, I couldn't go to the BSC meeting. Not unless I just rode off, completely disobeying her. And that would make Mama and Daddy (not to mention Aunt Cecelia) very mad. I knew I couldn't go without talking to my parents first.

"Can I at least call Kristy to tell her I won't be attending the meeting?" I asked Aunt Dictator. "That *is* the responsible thing to do."

My aunt let me make the call.

"Hi, Kristy," I said. "Guess what. I'm really sorry, but Aunt Cecelia won't allow me to come to the meeting today. I was ten minutes late getting back from the Rodowskys' and my aunt blew a fuse."

"Over ten minutes?"

"Yes. Can you believe it?"

"No. That's so unfair!"

"Listen, Kristy. Can you do something for me?" I lowered my voice even though I didn't need to. Aunt Dictator had taken Becca and Squirt into another room. "Can you call me a lot during the meeting? It'll make me look like you can't get along without me."

"Sure," replied Kristy. I knew she was smiling. That kind of thing appeals to her. "Your aunt'll think *you're* the BSC president!"

"Oh, thank you!" I told her.

Boy, did my friends live up to their promises. Our phone rang *fourteen* times between five-thirty and six o'clock.

By the third call, which was from Stacey, I

whispered, "Aren't you guys tying up the club phone? I don't want to make you do that."

"No. We're tying up the Kishis' phone. We're taking turns going down to the kitchen and using the phone there," Stacey told me.

"Oh, okay." Then I raised my voice for Aunt Cecelia's benefit. "No, tell Mrs. Hobart I won't be able to sit then. I have a dance class that afternoon."

By 6:00, Aunt Cecelia had had it up to *here*. (Picture me holding my hand to my chin.) She couldn't believe all the phone calls, but there wasn't much she could do about them — except not forbid me to attend another meeting, and she wouldn't do that again. Aunt Cecelia might be a jerk, but she's no fool.

After dinner that night, I just *casually* mentioned to Mama and Daddy that Aunt Cecelia and I were having some trouble, but I made it sound like no big deal, so my parents didn't seem upset. They didn't even talk to Aunt Cecelia (at least, I don't think they did).

Aunt Cecelia and I were locked into an awful game now. I'd do something, she'd do something back, neither of us was happy — and Mama and Daddy hardly had any idea what was going on. They were too busy with their jobs and their grown-up lives.

That night, Aunt Dictator came into my room and announced, "We have *got* to do something about your hair." I guess she was still mad about the fourteen phone calls.

Overbearing pig, I thought. I wanted to say those words to her face, but instead I said, "You can do whatever you want as long as Madame Noelle will approve."

Aunt Cecelia paused. For some reason, Mme. Noelle is practically a goddess to my aunt. I guess because I have come so far with my ballet — dancing lead roles and stuff.

Even so, Aunt Dictator was only slightly daunted. She got out a jar of cream, a brush, and some other things, and gave me the most awful hairdo possible. Fortunately, it was severe, so it was great for ballet. My hair would *never* be in my eyes. It couldn't escape the trap Aunt Cecelia had put it in.

"There," said my aunt. "Now you're someone I can be proud of."

Because of my *hair?*

I ran downstairs to complain to Mama and Daddy, but they were talking seriously about a problem Mama was having at work. They looked dead tired, too.

When they glanced up at me, standing in the doorway to the living room, all they said was, "Did you do something to your hair, Jessi?"

I left them alone. I didn't tell them what was really going on — that Aunt Cecelia was running our lives, and ruining mine.

CHAPTER 13

It was the evening of the science fair. I was so excited, you'd think *I'd* entered a project in it. (Well, in a way I had.) Anyway, the kids who were entering had to arrive at Stoney-brook Elementary by six-thirty in order to set up. The fair itself began at seven-thirty.

So at six-thirty, there were Stacey and Charlotte, Mal and Margo, Kristy and David Michael, Jackie and me, and a whole lot of kids and their parents or brothers or sisters or grandparents. Actually, Jackie and I had arrived at 6:20 to make sure we got our table staked out.

Now, at nearly seven o'clock, the all-purpose room was noisy and busy. All around Jackie and me were sighs of relief (when things went right) and groans (when things went wrong). Kids walked by carrying everything from huge pumpkins to complicated electrical things. I could hear the sounds of gears turning, tools tinkering, and video equipment. The all-purpose room was a pretty exciting place to be in.

"How do you feel, Jackie?" I asked him.

His volcano was loaded up and ready to explode. The "Welcome to the World of Volcanic Activity" sign was hung on the front of his desk. His pointer was in his hand.

"Fine," he replied, but he sounded nervous. "Listen to this: Igneous rocks are born from fire, the molting — "

"Molten," I corrected him.

"The molten rock that lies several feet — "

"Miles."

"Okay. Several miles below the surface of our wonderful earth."

"Just *our earth*, Jackie. Don't overdo it."

Jackie nodded miserably.

Seven-thirty. The all-purpose room had really filled up. Teachers and parents and families and friends were pouring in.

"Look!" cried Jackie. "There are Mom and Dad and Archie and Shea!"

Boy, did Jackie seem relieved.

The Rodowskys made a beeline for The World of Volcanic Activity.

"Your project looks great, son," exclaimed Jackie's father.

"Yeah, it really does," Shea managed to admit.

"You know what?" I said. "I think I'm going to look around at the other projects before the judging begins. Jackie, you stay here and answer questions — but don't set the volcano off, okay?"

Jackie laughed. "Okay." He was beginning to feel pleased with himself. Even Shea hadn't seen the volcano explode. Jackie couldn't wait for the big moment. He wanted to prove something to Shea who, as his big brother, was always several steps ahead of him.

I walked slowly around the room, looking at the displays and experiments. I saw a model of a human heart made from Play-Doh (I think). I saw a small-scale "dinosaur war." I saw an impressive project about the Ice Age. I saw Charlotte's plants with her charts and graphs. One plant was considerably more healthy-looking than the other two, which were sort of scraggly.

"Which plant is that?" I asked, pointing to the full, green one.

"Guess," she said.

"The one that listened to classical music."

"Wrong." Charlotte grinned. "It's the Duran Duran plant. I'm not sure why. Maybe they were just really *fresh* seeds."

114

I laughed, and continued my walk through the exhibits. When I got back to Jackie's display, I found his family preparing to take a look around, so I said I'd stay with Jackie.

The volcano attracted a lot of attention.

"Neat! What's that?" asked a curly-headed boy.

"A volcano," said Jackie proudly. "It can *erupt*. It makes ash and lava go everywhere. It's really messy."

"Can I see?" asked the boy.

Jackie's face fell. "Sorry. I can only make it explode once. I have to wait until the judges are here. You can see it then."

"Okay," said the boy, looking disappointed.

A few seconds later two girls walked by.

"A volcano!" exclaimed one. "Hey, I've always wondered. What *does* make a volcano?"

Jackie was prepared. "Igneous rocks are born from fire . . ." He said the entire speech without one mistake. I gave him the thumbs-up sign.

The girl frowned. "But *why*," she went on, "do igneous rocks do that? I mean, why does heat make a volcano erupt?"

Jackie was stumped. That wasn't part of his speech. And he couldn't demonstrate the volcano to the girls, either.

Just when I was beginning to feel bad, my

own family showed up. Well, Mama and Daddy and Becca did. Squirt was at home with Aunt Dictator. Becca had come because she wanted to see Charlotte's experiment, and my parents were there because of the volcano they'd been hearing about.

I began to feel better.

At eight o'clock, an announcement came over the PA system.

"Attention, please. May I have your attention? The judging will now begin. All participants in the science fair prepare to demonstrate and explain your projects to the judges. Visitors, please stand at the back of the room during the judging."

"That was our *prin*cipal," Jackie informed me. (You'd have thought the President of the United States had just spoken.)

"Good luck, Jackie," I said. "I know you'll do fine. When it's time to make the volcano erupt, tell the judges you have to call me to light the match because you're not allowed to do that yourself."

Jackie swallowed and nodded. I joined my family at the back of the room.

The judging began.

Two women and a man walked solemnly from table to table. They looked each project over. They requested demonstrations. They asked questions.

Asked questions? Oh, no! Jackie couldn't talk about anything that wasn't in his speech. I hoped fervently that the judges would be so impressed with his demonstration that they wouldn't ask him any questions.

Tick, tick, tick. It was almost eight-thirty.

At last the judges reached The World of Volcanic Activity. I saw Jackie whisper something to one of the women. Then he saw me in the crowd and motioned for me to come forward. I did so, matches in hand.

"This," said Jackie as I reached his table, "is Jessi. She's my helper. She has to light the match for me."

(The judges smiled.)

I lit the match, told everyone to stand back, and tossed the match in the volcano. Jackie threw his hands in the air and cried, "The miracle of a volcano comes to life before our very eyes!"

PHOO! Lava was everywhere! It almost spattered the judges. Then it settled into a nice gooey flow down the sides of the volcano. The judges looked extremely impressed.

I stood to the side as Jackie made his speech, using the pointer.

The judges nodded and smiled.

And then the questions began.

"How," asked the man, "is the crater of a volcano created?"

"Um," said Jackie. He looked at me, but I couldn't help him. "Um," he said again. "I don't know." At least he didn't admit that I'd practically done the project for him.

"Well . . . what happens to the lava when it has flowed out of the crater?" asked one of the women.

"It — it's very hot . . ." Jackie said lamely.

I looked at the ground. This was my fault. I felt terrible as I watched the judges make notations on their pads of paper. They walked on to the last project of the fair without even telling Jackie, "Good work," or "Nice going."

I went back to my parents and waited guiltily and nervously for the results of the fair to be announced.

"Jackie's project was great!" Dad said to me. "I've never seen such a thing. You really helped him."

A little too much, I thought.

Several minutes later, another announcement crackled over the loudspeaker. "The judges," said the principal, "have reached their decisions." (The judges were standing in the center of the room.) "They have chosen first-, second-, and third-place winners. When the winners are announced, will they please receive their ribbons from the judges? Thank you." There was a pause. Then the principal continued. "Third prize goes to Charlotte Johanssen for her project entitled 'The Power of Music.' "

Applause broke out. Charlotte, looking shy but pleased, edged over to the judges, received her yellow ribbon, and scurried back to her table, where she proudly attached the ribbon to the sign she'd made for her project.

The next two winners were announced. They went to kids I didn't know. I sought out Kristy, Mal, and my other friends in the crowd. Except for Stacey, they looked as disappointed as I felt.

But nobody looked more disappointed than Jackie, even though an Honorable Mention ribbon was already being fastened to his desk. (Every kid except the three winners was given an Honorable Mention.) The Rodowskys and I crowded around The World of Volcanic Activity.

"Don't be too upset, honey," Mrs. Rodowsky told Jackie.

I had to speak up. "He has a right to be upset," I said.

Mr. and Mrs. Rodowsky turned to me.

"Why?" they asked at the same time.

"Because — because I gave him so much help with his project that he really didn't do much of it himself."

"Yeah," said Jackie, giving me the evil eyeball.

"I'm really sorry," I went on. "I just wanted him to win. He's always saying he's no good at anything, or that he has bad luck. I wanted him to see that he *can* be a winner. I guess I went about it all wrong, though."

Mr. and Mrs. Rodowsky were really nice. They understood what had happened. I got the feeling that they might have done things like this for Jackie in the past. Mr. Rodowsky even admitted to building the glass and wood box for the volcano himself. (Well, with a *teeny* bit of help from Jackie.)

But Jackie, who's usually so easygoing and sunny, continued to scowl at me. "I just wanted to have fun," he said. "That was all. I just wanted to make a volcano erupt."

"Jackie, Jessi apologized to you," his father said gently.

"I know." Jackie finally managed a smile. But it quickly turned to a frown. "Oh, no," he muttered. "Here come John, Ian, and Danny. They're going to laugh at me. I just know it."

But the three boys who approached us looked excited.

"Jackie," said one, "your volcano was totally rad. Make it explode again!"

"Yeah," said another. "That was so cool."

Jackie explained why he couldn't "explode" the volcano again.

"Oh, well," said the boys. "It was still awesome." They started to walk away. "See you in school on Monday!" one called over his shoulder.

Jackie grinned at me like the Cheshire Cat. "I don't believe it!" he cried.

Mr. and Mrs. Rodowsky were smiling, too. "You know," said Jackie's mom, "there'll be another science fair next year. Jessi, maybe you could try helping Jackie again."

"I don't think so," I said. "I better not."

"Good," replied Jackie. "Because if I'm going to lose, I want to do it all by myself!"

We laughed, even Shea and Archie. But while I was laughing, I was thinking about something. I needed to talk to my parents. And I needed to talk to them badly.

CHAPTER 14

I left the Rodowskys and searched for my parents in the crowded all-purpose room. I finally found them at Charlotte's table, along with Becca, Charlotte's parents, Stacey, and of course, Charlotte.

I pulled my mother aside. "Mama? Can we go home now?"

"What's the matter, honey? Don't you feel well?" Mama's hand immediately went to my forehead. "No fever," she murmured.

"I feel fine," I told her. "I'm not sick. But I need to talk to you and Daddy. It's about Jackie and — and Aunt Cecelia and some other things. Please can we leave?"

"Of course we can." Mama looked alarmed.

We couldn't leave right away, though. Saying good-bye took awhile. Becca had to congratulate Charlotte one more time and finger the prized yellow ribbon. Then I ran into Kristy.

122

"Sorry about Jackie," she said sincerely.

"Thanks," I replied. "Sorry about David Michael."

Kristy smiled. "Thank you. But it's funny — he doesn't seem upset at all."

At last my family had made our way out to our car. As we drove home, Mama said, "Becca, Jessi wants to have a talk about some things with Daddy and me, so when we get to our house, could you keep Squirt and Aunt Cecelia company for awhile and let us have some privacy?"

"Okay." Becca sounded like she was on her way to the guillotine.

At home, Mama made tea, and she and Daddy and I sat at the kitchen table and sipped it.

"Now," said Mama, "tell us what's happened."

"Okay," I said, drawing in a breath. "It isn't something that *just* happened; it's something that's been going on for awhile. Only I didn't realize it — I mean, I didn't realize my part in it — until tonight, when Jackie didn't win a prize at the science fair."

My parents nodded, but they looked puzzled.

"See, this is what happened," I went on. "Jackie told me he thought it would be fun to

123

build a volcano. He likes messy things. He also said the school science fair was coming up. So I pushed him into entering. . . . And then I did his whole project for him."

"You what?" said Daddy.

"I did almost everything. I researched volcanoes. I made him memorize that speech. I even lettered the sign for his project. It was as if I didn't trust him. I treated him like a baby. I didn't listen to him. I just forged ahead and did everything my way, thinking it was better."

"Well, you certainly seem to have recognized your faults," said Daddy.

"Did you apologize to the Rodowskys?" asked Mama.

I nodded. "But that isn't all. See, there's Aunt Cecelia, too. Becca and I," (I had *not* planned to say this) "we call her Aunt Dictator. She is running our lives. She moved in here and she tells us what to do and what not to do. Or she does things for us. And she never listens to us and she certainly doesn't trust us. Do you know that she once wouldn't let me go to a BSC meeting because I was ten minutes late getting home and hadn't called her? I'd have called if I was going to be later than that — but not for ten minutes."

"Honey, why didn't you tell us about that?" asked Mama.

"Well, I did try to call Daddy at work," I admitted, "but Ed couldn't reach him. He said you were out of the office, Daddy. And then, well, Mama, I know your job is a big adjustment. I guess I just didn't want to bother you with Aunt Cecelia problems. You either, Daddy. She's your sister."

Mama and Daddy were silent for a moment. Then Daddy said, "I think it's time for a family conference."

(I knew he was going to say that.)

"Okay," I agreed. I guessed I could face Aunt Cecelia with Mama and Daddy and Becca around me.

Aunt Cecelia had just finished putting Squirt to bed, and she and Becca joined us in the kitchen. Mama poured tea for Aunt Cecelia and gave Becca a cup of juice.

Becca looked at me with eyes that were question marks.

"Cecelia," Daddy began, "it seems that Jessi hasn't been very happy lately. Becca, either. They feel . . . they feel that you don't trust them. They *are* big enough to do quite a few things on their own. We've been giving the girls a lot of responsibility. They're able to care

125

for Squirt and to take care of themselves. But they think that you want to do things for them — things *they're* capable of doing."

Aunt Cecelia's face turned stiff. "Perhaps you don't need me, then."

"Oh, yes, we do," Mama was quick to say. "The girls can't care for Squirt while they're in school, and — sorry, girls — but neither of them is much of a cook."

"I, um, I can understand how it happened," I spoke up. "I mean, why you took over, Aunt Cecelia. It's easy to do. I completely took over with Jackie and his volcano." (I had to tell the science-fair story again.) "But the thing was, I just wanted to show him that I care. I wanted him to feel good about himself."

"And *I* only wanted to show you that *I* care," Aunt Cecelia said. "I want you girls to grow up to be kind, responsible, neat, and polite. You know, it's an awful thing to have to say, but sometimes black people have to work twice as hard to prove themselves. It isn't fair, but that's the way it is — sometimes."

"That's kind of the way it is with Jackie, too," I said thoughtfully. "He's not stupid. He's smart. And he's kind and funny and a lot of other nice things. But he's a klutz, and that's how most people see him. So he has to

126

work twice as hard to prove himself."

Silence. Then Aunt Cecelia, looking pained, said, "As long as we're bearing our souls, I confess something else. I was afraid I wouldn't be as good a sitter as you, Jessi."

"You *were?*" That was the last thing I'd expected to hear. "But you blamed *me* when Becca was stranded on the island."

"I know, but I shouldn't have. I needed something or someone to blame for that tragedy, and you were it. But I know you've been taking care of your brother and sister — not to mention all the kids you sit for — for quite awhile now, and you're an expert. I wasn't sure I could live up to you.

"On the other hand," Aunt Cecelia continued, her voice changing, growing stronger, "there's a little matter I need to mention to your parents. I think I've kept quiet about it long enough now, don't you?"

Dum da-dum dum. The practical jokes.

Becca and I nodded, but we couldn't look at anyone, not even at each other. We stared into our cups.

"What is it?" asked Daddy warily.

"Ever since I got here," Aunt Cecelia replied, "from the very beginning, I've found spiders — fake ones — in my bed, shaving cream in my shoes, and more, plenty more."

"Girls," said Mama warningly.

"Well, we were mad. She was already taking over. She was our *baby*-sitter, ordering us around, making up rules. I don't need a sitter!" I cried. "I *am* a sitter. And a good one . . . like Aunt Cecelia said," I couldn't help pointing out. This time I looked directly at my aunt and held her gaze.

"Okay. Obviously we've got some problems to work out," said Daddy. He turned to his sister. "Cecelia, I understand that you feel responsible for the girls, but they're used to certain things. For instance, Jessi never misses a meeting of the Baby-sitters Club. Not unless she has a special dance rehearsal or there's an emergency. We don't withhold that privilege as a punishment. I think that from now on, the girls should tell their mother or me about any plans they have. They can do this daily or weekly; we'll see what works best. We'll approve — or not approve — their plans, and then we'll tell you their schedules. Fair enough?"

"Fair enough," replied Aunt Cecelia. I could see her relax a little.

"Fair enough?" Daddy asked Becca and me.

"Yup," we agreed.

"Furthermore, the girls should be allowed to do the things we already trust them to do —

fix their hair, choose their own clothes, that sort of thing," added Mama. "And perhaps," she went on, "it might be helpful if Cecelia is referred to simply as the children's *aunt*, not their sitter."

Aunt Cecelia smiled. "That sounds nice."

"Now," said Daddy, "there's a little matter of a punishment."

"A punishment?" squeaked Becca. "For who?"

"For *whom*," Aunt Cecelila corrected her gently.

"For you and your sister," Mama said sternly. "For spiders and shaving cream and I don't know what all."

"Just a moment," interrupted my aunt. "Could I speak to you in private?" she asked my parents.

"Of course," they replied.

Becca and I escaped then. We didn't know what was going on, but we were glad to get out of there. That night, I slept like, well, like Squirt!

CHAPTER 15

Monday afternoon. Five-twenty-eight. Time for another BSC meeting.

We were all gathered. Kristy was sitting in the director's chair, visor on, pencil over her ear, watching Claud's digital clock, waiting for it to hit five-thirty on the nose.

Claudia was foraging for junk food.

My friends and I were dressed in typical outfits. *Typical*, but not necessarily traditional. For instance, Stacey was wearing tight black pants that reached just above her ankles, and sported a column of four silvery buttons at the bottoms. (The buttons were just for show, I think.) Over the pants she was wearing a *long* (past her knees) blue jacket made of soft material. Under that she was wearing a sleeveless blouse. Now that was unusual.

Claud was wearing a fake leopard-skin vest, a fairly tame blouse, and blue leggings. She had made her jewelry herself — five papier-mâché bracelets that were painted in soft desert colors.

Mary Anne and Dawn had traded outfits, which they do pretty often. That's one nice thing about having a stepsister who's your best friend and also about your size. They were both dressed colorfully, and trendily, but not as wildly as Claud and Stace.

Then there was Kristy in her jeans and turtleneck. And finally Mal and me, also in jeans, but wearing (if I do say so myself) pretty *fresh* sweat shirts. And Mal had been allowed to buy high-top sneakers with beaded designs on the sides!

Click. The clock turned to five-thirty.

"Order, please," said Kristy. "Treasurer, it's dues day."

Groan, groan, groan. We all produced our dues. Stacey counted the treasury money and looked pleased.

Before Kristy could even say, "Any club business?" the phone rang.

"Good sign!" she exclaimed, as Dawn answered it.

"Good afternoon, the Baby-sitters Club," said Dawn. Then, "Hi, Mrs. Newton. . . . Friday? I'll check and call you right back."

We arranged that job plus two others before things calmed down.

Then Mal said, "Did everyone survive the science fair?"

"Just barely," I replied.

"David Michael is ecstatic," reported Kristy.

"Over an Honorable Mention?" asked Dawn. "Anyone who didn't win got an Honorable Mention."

Kristy smiled. "I know. That doesn't matter to David Michael, though. He's just thrilled with the idea of a prize — any prize. He wouldn't even leave the ribbon on his project at the fair. He brought it home on Friday night, slept with it, and carried it around with him on Saturday until Watson suggested having it mounted. Now it's hanging over his bed. You'd think it was the Pulitzer Prize."

"That's sweet," said Mary Anne. "I'm glad David Michael is so happy. You know, it's funny what these fairs do for different kids."

"Yeah," said Mal. "Margo's proud of her project, but not the Honorable Mention. It doesn't mean much to her. She just wants everyone to see Barbie on the moon."

"What about Charlotte?" I asked Stacey.

Stacey rolled her eyes. "Oh, wow. You should see her. She is in science heaven. She found out that the names of the three winners will appear in the *Stoneybrook News*. She's gotten a huge boost of self-confidence."

132

"Jackie's reaction is a little different from everyone else's," I spoke up. "He doesn't care about the Honorable Mention, either. But once he got over being humiliated when he couldn't answer the judges' questions, he returned to his usual self. He doesn't want me to help him with next year's project, though."

"I don't blame him," said Kristy.

"Neither do I," I answered.

Then I told the BSC members what had happened Friday night when my family and I had gotten home from the fair.

"What did your aunt want to talk to your parents about in private?" asked Claud.

"I have no idea. That was three days ago and I haven't heard a word about it. I'm afraid to ask."

"You don't think she's leaving, do you?" asked Mal suddenly.

I paused. Then I said, "Gosh. . . . I don't know. I thought we'd worked everything out. We talked about how sometimes people take over when they just want to show they care. The way I did with Jackie and his project. And we set up some rules. No. I don't think she's leaving."

You know what was weird? Just then, a little part of me *hoped* she wasn't leaving. If she did, what would we do about Squirt while Mama worked? And who would be around to care *about* me (not for me) in the afternoons? The thought surprised me.

The phone rang then and we took a job call, and then another. When silence fell again, Dawn said, "Guess what? I'm going to California on our next school vacation. I'll get to see Dad and Jeff."

"That's *great*," said Kristy. "You know where Shannon Kilbourne is going?" (She paused dramatically.) "To Hawaii."

There was a huge chorus of "Oh, wows," and, "That is *so* fresh," and, "Boy, is she lucky."

Mal looked downcast. "I don't think I'll be going *any*where for awhile. Dad's company is in trouble. He said he heard the president is going to lay off about half the people who work there. Dad says he thinks he'll be one of them."

"But he might not be," I pointed out.

"That's true. I guess there's no point in worrying about it unless it happens."

On that somber note, the meeting broke up and I rode home. I forgot about Mal and her father and his job, and began to feel cheerful. That was because this time I knew there would be no disapproving Aunt Cecelia waiting to pounce on me when I got home. There would

134

be (I hoped) just a regular aunt who was probably making dinner and trying to entertain Squirt at the same time.

I was right on both counts.

When I entered our house I saw my aunt at the stove, stirring things in pots. Sitting at her feet was Squirt, who was banging frying pans with a wooden spoon and looking pretty pleased with himself.

"Hi, Aunt Cecelia," I was saying, just as Becca appeared next to me and gestured wildly but silently for me to follow her. So I did. I followed her upstairs to her room, where at last she found her voice — sort of.

"Jes — Jes — Look at — I mean, see what — "

"Becca, what on earth is the matter?" I asked her.

"Go look at my slippers," was her reply.

I opened Becca's closet door, turned on the light, bent down, and saw that her slippers were filled with shaving cream.

"I almost put them *on*," she said, horrified. "Then, I needed my flashlight, so I pulled back my bedspread" (Becca keeps her flashlight under her pillow) "and I found *this* in my bed." My sister held up a huge, disgusting plastic fly. "You didn't do these things, did you?" she asked, narrowing her eyes at me.

"Of course not," I replied. "I bet it was . . ."

"Aunt Cecelia!" we said together.

Then we bolted for my room. I found shaving cream in my slippers and a furry mouse (fake) under my pillow, and discovered that my bed had been short-sheeted.

Becca and I just looked at each other.

Then we heard gentle laughter. We turned around. Aunt Cecelia was standing in my doorway, holding Squirt on her hip.

"I guess we're even now," said my aunt.

I couldn't help smiling. "I guess so."

"Yeah," agreed Becca.

"Aunt Cecelia . . . I'm sorry," I told her. "We weren't very nice to you. We didn't give you much of a chance."

"I didn't give you two much of a chance, either," she replied. "I did move in and take over. But that's going to change now."

"Hey, Aunt Cecelia, want to hear a joke?" asked Becca, which I knew was her way of apologizing.

"Of course I do. Come downstairs and tell it to me while I finish dinner. . . . Um, Jessi, you can watch Squirt for me."

"Thanks," I said.

So we returned to the kitchen and Becca told Aunt Cecelia a joke that I used to tell Becca.

"See, a long time ago, there was this Viking," Becca began. "And his name was Rudolph the Red. And one day he looked up at the sky and said to his wife, 'It's going to rain today.' And his wife said, 'No, it's not. The sky is blue and the sun is shining.' And Rudolph said, 'But it's still going to rain,' and his wife said, 'Is not,' and Rudolph said, 'Is too.' So finally his wife said, 'How can you tell?' and her husband replied, 'Because Rudolph the Red knows rain, dear.' "

Aunt Cecelia let out a burst of laughter like I'd never heard. Not from her, anyway. So we all began to laugh, even Squirt, although he hadn't understood the joke, of course.

And that was how Mama and Daddy found the four of us when they came home from work that night. All together in the kitchen, laughing.

"Well," said Daddy, "I think this household is finally settling down."

"Yup," I agreed. And I was pretty happy with the way things had turned out.

Later that night, I tore up the list of mean things to do to Aunt Cecelia.

Dear Reader,

My sister Jane and I had lots of baby-sitters when we were growing up. We didn't like some of them, especially the old ones who smelled funny. But we did have some favorites. One of them was my friend Beth's older brother Johnny. He was the one who taught us how to burp. Another one, also named Johnny, invented bowling on the stairs (I wrote about that in a Baby-sitters Little Sister book). My best baby-sitters had a sense of humor, and did fun things with us. I tried to remember that a few years later when I became a baby-sitter myself.

Happy reading,

Ann M. Martin

L. GODWIN

Ann M. Martin

About the Author

ANN MATTHEWS MARTIN was born on August 12, 1955. She grew up in Princeton, NJ, with her parents and her younger sister, Jane.

Although Ann used to be a teacher and then an editor of children's books, she's now a full-time writer. She gets the ideas for her books from many different places. Some are based on personal experiences. Others are based on childhood memories and feelings. Many are written about contemporary problems or events.

All of Ann's characters, even the members of the Baby-sitters Club, are made up. (So is Stoneybrook.) But many of her characters are based on real people. Sometimes Ann names her characters after people she knows, other times she chooses names she likes.

In addition to the Baby-sitters Club books, Ann Martin has written many other books for children. Her favorite is *Ten Kids, No Pets* because she loves big families and she loves animals. Her favorite Baby-sitters Club book is *Kristy's Big Day*. (By the way, Kristy is her favorite baby-sitter!)

Ann M. Martin now lives in New York with her cats, Gussie and Woody. Her hobbies are reading, sewing, and needlework — especially making clothes for children.

Notebook Pages

This Baby-sitters Club book belongs to _____ .

I am _____ years old and in the _____

grade.

The name of my school is _____ .

I got this BSC book from _____ .

I started reading it on _____ and

finished reading it on _____ .

The place where I read most of this book is _____ .

My favorite part was when _____ .

If I could change anything in the story, it might be the part when

_____ .

My favorite character in the Baby-sitters Club is _____ .

The BSC member I am most like is _____

because _____ .

If I could write a Baby-sitters Club book it would be about ___

_____ .

#36 Jessi's Baby-sitter

Jessi does not like it one bit when Aunt Cecelia becomes her baby-sitter. She thinks she's too old for a baby-sitter! I think a kid is too old for a baby-sitter when he/she turns _____ years old. The best baby-sitter I ever had was _____ _____ . This person was the best baby-sitter because _____ _____ _____ . Some cool things that baby-sitters can do are _____ _____ . One thing a baby-sitter should never do is _____ . If I *had* to have someone in my family watch over me (like Jessi's aunt), I would want it to be _____ because _____ . If I had to have a member of the BSC baby-sit for me, I would want it to be ____ _____ because _____ _____ .

JESSI'S

this is me at age four.

Me with my new baby brother.

I'm always happy when I'm dancing.

SCRAPBOOK

Matt and Haley Braddock, two of my favorite charges.

My family — Daddy and Mama Becca, me, Aunt Cecelia and Squirt.

Read all the books
about **Jessi**
in the Baby-sitters Club series
by Ann M. Martin

THE BABY-SITTERS CLUB®

The best friends you'll ever have!

Collect 'em all!

by Ann M. Martin

❏ MG43388-1	#1	Kristy's Great Idea	$3.50
❏ MG43387-3	#10	Logan Likes Mary Anne!	$3.99
❏ MG43717-8	#15	Little Miss Stoneybrook...and Dawn	$3.50
❏ MG43722-4	#20	Kristy and the Walking Disaster	$3.50
❏ MG43347-4	#25	Mary Anne and the Search for Tigger	$3.50
❏ MG42498-X	#30	Mary Anne and the Great Romance	$3.50
❏ MG42508-0	#35	Stacey and the Mystery of Stoneybrook	$3.50
❏ MG44082-9	#40	Claudia and the Middle School Mystery	$3.25
❏ MG43574-4	#45	Kristy and the Baby Parade	$3.50
❏ MG44969-9	#50	Dawn's Big Date	$3.50
❏ MG44968-0	#51	Stacey's Ex-Best Friend	$3.50
❏ MG44966-4	#52	Mary Anne + 2 Many Babies	$3.50
❏ MG44967-2	#53	Kristy for President	$3.25
❏ MG44965-6	#54	Mallory and the Dream Horse	$3.25
❏ MG44964-8	#55	Jessi's Gold Medal	$3.25
❏ MG45657-1	#56	Keep Out, Claudia!	$3.50
❏ MG45658-X	#57	Dawn Saves the Planet	$3.50
❏ MG45659-8	#58	Stacey's Choice	$3.50
❏ MG45660-1	#59	Mallory Hates Boys (and Gym)	$3.50
❏ MG45662-8	#60	Mary Anne's Makeover	$3.50
❏ MG45663-6	#61	Jessi's and the Awful Secret	$3.50
❏ MG45664-4	#62	Kristy and the Worst Kid Ever	$3.50
❏ MG45665-2	#63	Claudia's Special Friend	$3.50
❏ MG45666-0	#64	Dawn's Family Feud	$3.50
❏ MG45667-9	#65	Stacey's Big Crush	$3.50
❏ MG47004-3	#66	Maid Mary Anne	$3.50
❏ MG47005-1	#67	Dawn's Big Move	$3.50
❏ MG47006-X	#68	Jessi and the Bad Baby-sitter	$3.50
❏ MG47007-8	#69	Get Well Soon, Mallory!	$3.50
❏ MG47008-6	#70	Stacey and the Cheerleaders	$3.50
❏ MG47009-4	#71	Claudia and the Perfect Boy	$3.50
❏ MG47010-8	#72	Dawn and the We Love Kids Club	$3.50
❏ MG47011-6	#73	Mary Anne and Miss Priss	$3.50
❏ MG47012-4	#74	Kristy and the Copycat	$3.50
❏ MG47013-2	#75	Jessi's Horrible Prank	$3.50
❏ MG47014-0	#76	Stacey's Lie	$3.50
❏ MG48221-1	#77	Dawn and Whitney, Friends Forever	$3.50

More titles... ▶

The Baby-sitters Club titles continued...

☐ MG48222-X	#78	Claudia and the Crazy Peaches	$3.50
☐ MG48223-8	#79	Mary Anne Breaks the Rules	$3.50
☐ MG48224-6	#80	Mallory Pike, #1 Fan	$3.50
☐ MG48225-4	#81	Kristy and Mr. Mom	$3.50
☐ MG48226-2	#82	Jessi and the Troublemaker	$3.50
☐ MG48235-1	#83	Stacey vs. the BSC	$3.50
☐ MG48228-9	#84	Dawn and the School Spirit War	$3.50
☐ MG48236-X	#85	Claudi Kishli, Live from WSTO	$3.50
☐ MG48227-0	#86	Mary Anne and Camp BSC	$3.50
☐ MG48237-8	#87	Stacey and the Bad Girls	$3.50
☐ MG22872-2	#88	Farewell, Dawn	$3.50
☐ MG22873-0	#89	Kristy and the Dirty Diapers	$3.50
☐ MG22874-9	#90	Welcome to the BSC, Abby	$3.50
☐ MG22875-1	#91	Claudia and the First Thanksgiving	$3.50
☐ MG22876-5	#92	Mallory's Christmas Wish	$3.50
☐ MG22877-3	#93	Mary Anne and the Memory Garden	$3.99
☐ MG22878-1	#94	Stacey McGill, Super Sitter	$3.99
☐ MG45575-3		Logan's Story Special Edition Readers' Request	$3.25
☐ MG47118-X		Logan Bruno, Boy Baby-sitter Special Edition Readers' Request	$3.50
☐ MG47756-0		Shannon's Story Special Edition	$3.50
☐ MG47686-6		The Baby-sitters Club Guide to Baby-sitting	$3.25
☐ MG47314-X		The Baby-sitters Club Trivia and Puzzle Fun Book	$2.50
☐ MG48400-1		BSC Portrait Collection: Claudia's Book	$3.50
☐ MG22864-1		BSC Portrait Collection: Dawn's Book	$3.50
☐ MG48399-4		BSC Portrait Collection: Stacey's Book	$3.50
☐ MG47151-1		The Baby-sitters Club Chain Letter	$14.95
☐ MG48295-5		The Baby-sitters Club Secret Santa	$14.95
☐ MG45074-3		The Baby-sitters Club Notebook	$2.50
☐ MG44783-1		The Baby-sitters Club Postcard Book	$4.95

Available wherever you buy books...or use this order form.

Scholastic Inc., P.O. Box 7502, 2931 E. McCarty Street, Jefferson City, MO 65102

Please send me the books I have checked above. I am enclosing $_____
(please add $2.00 to cover shipping and handling). Send check or money order–no cash or
C.O.D.s please.

Name _____ Birthdate_____

Address _____

City_____ State/Zip _____

Please allow four to six weeks for delivery. Offer good in the U.S. only. Sorry, mail orders are not available
to residents of Canada. Prices subject to change.

THE BABY-SITTERS CLUB®

by Ann M. Martin

Collect and read these exciting BSC Super Specials, Mysteries, and Super Mysteries along with your favorite Baby-sitters Club books!

BSC Super Specials

❑ BBK44240-6	Baby-sitters on Board! Super Special #1	$3.95
❑ BBK44239-2	Baby-sitters' Summer Vacation Super Special #2	$3.95
❑ BBK43973-1	Baby-sitters' Winter Vacation Super Special #3	$3.95
❑ BBK42493-9	Baby-sitters' Island Adventure Super Special #4	$3.95
❑ BBK43575-2	California Girls! Super Special #5	$3.95
❑ BBK43576-0	New York, New York! Super Special #6	$3.95
❑ BBK44963-X	Snowbound! Super Special #7	$3.95
❑ BBK44962-X	Baby-sitters at Shadow Lake Super Special #8	$3.95
❑ BBK45661-X	Starring The Baby-sitters Club! Super Special #9	$3.95
❑ BBK45674-1	Sea City, Here We Come! Super Special #10	$3.95
❑ BBK47015-9	The Baby-sitters Remember Super Special #11	$3.95
❑ BBK48308-0	Here Come the Bridesmaids! Super Special #12	$3.95

BSC Mysteries

❑ BAI44084-5	#1 Stacey and the Missing Ring	$3.50
❑ BAI44085-3	#2 Beware Dawn!	$3.50
❑ BAI44799-8	#3 Mallory and the Ghost Cat	$3.50
❑ BAI44800-5	#4 Kristy and the Missing Child	$3.50
❑ BAI44801-3	#5 Mary Anne and the Secret in the Attic	$3.50
❑ BAI44961-3	#6 The Mystery at Claudia's House	$3.50
❑ BAI44960-5	#7 Dawn and the Disappearing Dogs	$3.50
❑ BAI44959-1	#8 Jessi and the Jewel Thieves	$3.50
❑ BAI44958-3	#9 Kristy and the Haunted Mansion	$3.50

More titles ➡

The Baby-sitters Club books continued...

Available wherever you buy books...or use this order form.

Scholastic Inc., P.O. Box 7502, 2931 East McCarty Street, Jefferson City, MO 65102-7502

Please send me the books I have checked above. I am enclosing $ _____
(please add $2.00 to cover shipping and handling). Send check or money order
— no cash or C.O.D.s please.

Name_____ Birthdate_____

Address _____

City_____ State/Zip_____

Please allow four to six weeks for delivery. Offer good in the U.S. only. Sorry, mail orders are not
available to residents of Canada. Prices subject to change.

BSCM795

THE BABY-SITTERS CLUB®

ALL NEW!

by Ann M. Martin

Meet the best friends you'll ever have!

Have you heard? The BSC has a new look
—and more great stuff than ever before.
An all-new scrapbook for each book's narrator!
A letter from Ann M. Martin! Fill-in pages to
personalize your copy! Order today!

☐ BBD22473-5	#1	**Kristy's Great Idea**	$3.50
☐ BBD22763-7	#2	**Claudia and the Phantom Phone Calls**	$3.99
☐ BBD25158-9	#3	**The Truth About Stacey**	$3.99
☐ BBD25159-7	#4	**Mary Anne Saves the Day**	$3.50
☐ BBD25160-0	#5	**Dawn and the Impossible Three**	$3.50
☐ BBD25161-9	#6	**Kristy's Big Day**	$3.50
☐ BBD25162-7	#7	**Claudia and Mean Janine**	$3.50
☐ BBD25163-5	#8	**Boy Crazy Stacey**	$3.50
☐ BBD25164-3	#9	**The Ghost at Dawn's House**	$3.99
☐ BBD25165-1	#10	**Logan Likes Mary Anne!**	$3.99
☐ BBD25166-X	#11	**Kristy and the Snobs**	$3.99
☐ BBD25167-8	#12	**Claudia and the New Girl**	$3.99

Available wherever you buy books, or use this order form.

Send orders to Scholastic Inc., P.O. Box 7500, 2931 East McCarty Street, Jefferson City, MO 65102.

Please send me the books I have checked above. I am enclosing $_____ (please add $2.00 to cover shipping and handling). Send check or money order—no cash or C.O.D.s please. Please allow four to six weeks for delivery. Offer good in the U.S.A. only. Sorry, mail orders are not available to residents in Canada. Prices subject to change.

Name_____ Birthdate ___/___/___
    First   Last   D / M / Y

Address_____

City_____ State_____ Zip_____

Telephone (____) _____ ☐ Boy ☐ Girl

Where did you buy this book? Bookstore ☐   Book Fair ☐
                                        Book Club ☐   Other ☐

SCHOLASTIC

BSCF995

What's the scoop with Dawn, Kristy, Mallory, and the other girls?

Be the first to know with G★I★R★L★ magazine!

Hey, Baby-sitters Club readers! Now you can be the first on the block to get in on the action of G★I★R★L★ It's an exciting new magazine that lets you dig in and read...

★ Upcoming selections from Ann Martin's Baby-sitters Club books
★ Fun articles on handling stress, turning dreams into great careers, making and keeping best friends, and much more
★ Plus, all the latest on new movies, books, music, and sports!

To get in on the scoop, just cut and mail this coupon today. And don't forget to tell all your friends about G★I★R★L★ magazine!

A neat offer for you...6 issues for only $15.00.

Sign up today -- this special offer ends July 1, 1996!

❑ **YES!** Please send me G★I★R★L★ magazine. I will receive six fun-filled issues for only $15.00. Enclosed is a check (no cash, please) made payable to G★I★R★L★ for $15.00.

Just fill in, cut out, and mail this coupon with your payment of $15.00 to: G★I★R★L★, c/o Scholastic Inc., 2931 East McCarty Street, Jefferson City, MO 65101.

Name _____

Address _____

City, State, ZIP _____

9013